Uncle Charles
Has Locked
Himself In

Georges Simenon

UNCLE CHARLES HAS LOCKED HIMSELF IN

TRANSLATED FROM THE FRENCH
BY HOWARD CURTIS

A Helen and Kurt Wolff Book

Harcourt Brace Jovanovich, Publishers

San Diego   New York   London

HBJ *FIC*

Copyright 1942 by Libraire Gallimard
English translation copyright © 1987 by Georges Simenon

All rights reserved. No part of this publication
may be reproduced or transmitted in any form or
by any means, electronic or mechanical, including
photocopy, recording, or any information storage
and retrieval system, without permission in
writing from the publisher. *R0057251157*

Requests for permission to make copies of any
part of the work should be mailed to:
Permissions, Harcourt Brace Jovanovich, Publishers,
Orlando, Florida 32887.

Library of Congress Cataloging-in-Publication Data
Simenon, Georges, 1903–
Uncle Charles has locked himself in.
Translation of: Oncle Charles s'est enfermé.
"A Helen and Kurt Wolff book."
I. Title.
PQ2637.I5306513   1987   843'.912   87-7609
ISBN 0-15-192685-9

Designed by G. B. D. Smith

Printed in the United States of America

First edition

A B C D E

Uncle Charles Has Locked Himself In

Chapter 1

IT WAS THE TIME OF YEAR WHEN DARKNESS FELL BY FOUR IN the afternoon.

Laurence got off the streetcar at the same time as the motorman, who would soon be turning around for the return trip. And there in front of her, as always, taking up as much space in her field of vision as the moon in the sky, Laurence saw the signal light of the grade crossing.

She pushed open the gate, which was cold and wet to the touch (it must have rained while she was at Céline's), and looked to right and left. She heard threatening noises and saw colored lights looming out of the darkness amid swirls of steam.

"Come on! Hurry up!" a man with a small flag shouted at her.

There were four or five tracks to cross, too many for comfort, what with the constant traffic of freight trains with tank cars from the oil refineries.

"One of these days . . ."

The same thought occurred to her each time she crossed the tracks and, with relief, opened the gate on the other side. From there on things were calmer: an almost deserted street of identical houses, an occasional street lamp, and only two shop windows—not even real shop windows, but the sort of tiny displays found in the windows of houses that doubled as shops in the suburbs.

Absentmindedly she passed Josse's, the pork butcher's, and had to turn and walk back. The bell clanged as she entered. Madame Josse, on her short legs, appeared from the back of the shop.

"Let me have half a pound of pâté."

"Is it still raining?" asked Madame Josse.

"It stopped while I was at my sister's. Are these pig's feet fresh?"

"Fresh this morning."

"Let me have a pound. I'm the only one who eats them."

Her own house was three doors down. As she searched for the key in her bag, she looked through the keyhole and saw that nobody was home: there was no light visible through the glass door of the kitchen, at the end of the hall.

The fire, however, was still going, and its warmth enveloped her as soon as she got in the front door. Before taking off her hat and coat, she stirred and stoked the fire, turned on the gas, then poured warm milk into the cat's saucer. Then she glanced at the alarm clock on the mantelpiece: it was not quite seven.

Laurence always took her time. She was too fat, too flabby, too easily out of breath, ever to hurry. Besides, didn't the others always manage to turn up only when dinner was ready?

Putting the pâté on a plate, she took a little taste of it, then went to get the cheese from the closet next to the oleander.

All the other kitchens on the street were identical: a small room at the end of the hall, looking onto a backyard with an outdoor toilet.

Only the Dupeux family's kitchen was different. The previous tenant had been a photographer, who had had a glass roof put over the backyard. It made for a curious room, half covered by a real ceiling, half covered by glass, with a brick

2

wall at the end, which they had simply painted when they moved in. They could eat dinner beneath the stars, if there were any, and the photographer's two oleanders were still in their corners, in their green tubs.

Laurence felt like eating another bite. When she was alone, she could happily have spent all her time eating. But at that moment the front door opened. She looked out. It was Camille, pushing her bicycle into the hall and taking off her coat and hat at the bamboo coatrack.

"Are we eating yet?" she asked, entering the kitchen.

"You can eat if you like. The others aren't home."

Camille, who was sensitive to the cold—Céline said it was because she didn't have enough blood—warmed her pale hands at the fire. She was wearing a navy-blue skirt and a light-blue sweater she had knit herself.

They heard a noise at the mailbox.

"Lulu's forgotten her key again!"

Lulu was the youngest. Her black dress was too tight and clung to her thin body. There were drops of water on her hair.

"Is it raining again?"

"Just started . . ." Lulu muttered, cutting herself a piece of pâté. "Is that all there is to eat?"

She was an assistant in a shoe store in the center of town, and there was always a vague smell of leather about her. As for Camille, she worked for a corset-maker.

"Wasn't your father on the streetcar?"

"If he had been, he'd be here by now, wouldn't he?"

Lulu sat down in a wicker armchair and opened a movie magazine at random.

The last of them arrived: Mauricette, the best dressed. She entered the kitchen without a word, went straight to the table, and sat down, as if determined to eat alone if the others still dithered.

3

Ten after seven. In the distance the din continued: train whistles, factory noises, the rattling of railroad cars.

"Here he is!" announced Laurence, as the front door opened again.

Out of habit, she glanced into the hall. The yellowing walls, painted in imitation of marble, were lighted by a single bulb with a colored-glass shade. Halfway along, the staircase began.

"He's carrying packages," she said in surprise.

"Who're the pig's feet for?" asked Lulu, sitting down at the table.

But her mother was still looking out at the hall.

"What on earth's he up to?"

It was quite the most remarkable thing that could have happened. Instead of taking off his hat and coat in the hall, Charles Dupeux was climbing the stairs, without so much as a glance toward the kitchen. They could all hear his rather furtive steps, which did not even pause on the second-floor landing.

"What's the date?" asked Laurence, looking at the calendar. "The twelfth . . . It isn't anyone's name day, is it?"

That might have explained it. Her husband might have bought presents and gone to hide them in the spare room.

Laurence always tended to see the funny side of things, particularly where her husband was concerned. So she was not especially worried. Yet, to hear better, she opened the kitchen door a little wider and stood there listening.

"What on earth's he up to this time?"

The implication was that Charles Dupeux was the sort of man who might do anything.

There was nothing on the third floor except the spare room and the attic.

"I bet he can't find the light switch. . . ."

4

They could hear him, burdened by his packages, groping at the walls and doors.

"Well, *I'm* eating!" said Lulu, decisively.

Mauricette was already eating, without saying a word, nibbling at her food as if disgusted by the absence of a table-cloth. The water for the coffee was coming to a boil.

"I wonder what he's doing up there. . . ."

He had not gone to the spare room, but into the attic. The floorboards were bare, and his steps echoed through the house. Then came a noise like the sound of furniture being dragged across the floor.

"Lulu . . . go and see what your father . . ."

"Why me?"

"Why not you?" retorted Mauricette.

Lulu went out, with her mouth full and rolling her hips as she had taken to doing in the past few weeks.

"Are you in there, Papa? . . . Papa! . . . Answer me! What are you doing?"

Downstairs, the others listened. Laurence felt like laughing, so absurd did the whole thing seem to her.

"What on earth's he up to?" she repeated.

"Papa! . . . Papa! . . ."

Lulu's voice had changed; it had taken on an anguished tone. She was banging at the door and trying to get it open.

Finally she came running down. Her hair had come loose, and there was a worried look in her eyes.

"What did he say?"

"Nothing. He won't answer."

"Do you know what he's doing?"

"Moving things around."

She looked at the others. Her mother was the least bothered and still felt like laughing.

"I always said he'd go completely mad one of these days."

5

"Mama!"

"Well, what of it? What can I do if he decides to go and lock himself in the attic? He'll come down when he's had enough."

She sat down at the table, placed some pig's feet on her plate and helped herself to a copious amount of mustard. Only Lulu, disturbed by what she had heard upstairs, remained standing.

"You ought to go and have a look," she said to Mauricette.

Strangely enough, Mauricette, who usually, as a matter of principle, never did what was asked of her, went up without protest.

"Are you there, Father? . . . Open the door!"

Camille was looking at the clock. Lulu noticed.

"Are you going out?"

"I've got my shorthand class."

It had been a curious whim of Camille's suddenly to take up shorthand, at the age of twenty, even though she had a job making corsets.

"Father! . . . At least say something . . . What are you doing in there? . . . Father!"

There was quite a long silence. Then they heard Mauricette's footsteps on the stairs. She stopped under the lamp in the hall to read something. When she came back into the kitchen, she placed a piece of paper on the table.

"Look!" She sighed.

"What is it?"

"A note he slid under the door."

Lulu read it aloud: "*Please leave me in peace!*"

Laurence laughed. It was not a nervous laugh; whenever she laughed, her pale flesh shook and her big breasts jogged up and down inside her blouse. She had never worn a brassiere; she said they choked her. Perhaps because of that, when you looked at her, you thought of warm milk. Her blond hair was never in place. Nor did her hats ever stay in place on her head, and none of her dresses seemed to fit.

"Well, if that's what he wants!" she sneered.

Camille was still looking anxiously at the clock, wondering if she dared . . .

"What are you waiting for?" asked Lulu. "We can see you're in a hurry to go."

"I have to be in class by eight."

"Well? Who's stopping you?"

Laurence did not interfere. Her daughters could do whatever they liked.

"Are you going out?" Camille asked Mauricette.

"Not yet."

Because Mauricette still had to get dressed up. She was not going to anything as ordinary as a shorthand class. For the next quarter of an hour, she could be heard moving about in her room, and the scent of cheap perfume wafted down into the hall. She was careful not to go back into the kitchen, in order not to show her made-up face.

"Mauricette!" her mother called out.

"What?"

She was already at the front door, afraid of being delayed.

"Could you stop in at your uncle Henri's . . ."

"What for?"

"To ask him if anything was the matter with your father today."

"All right."

"Will you do it?"

She was already outside and closing the door behind her. Only Lulu was left, but not for long.

"Where are *you* going?" asked her mother, seeing her put on her beret.

"To the movies."

"Have you got money?"

For a moment, Lulu's eyes came to a standstill in her thin face, but the moment passed, and she stammered in a low voice, as if lying: "Yes . . ."

Outside, having no money, she did not catch the streetcar. She ran across the tracks at the grade crossing, where the big round light of an approaching train, wheezing steam, could be seen. The gate banged shut.

"One of these days . . ."

She was walking fast. Her high heels made a dry tapping sound on the sidewalk. Her coat sailed out behind her, and wisps of hair escaped from under her beret.

She was almost alone on the street. From time to time, a word broke from her, part of the half-thought, half-spoken monologue she kept up as she walked. She crossed Boïeldieu Bridge. As she reached the other side, a figure emerged from the shadows, and a man's arm slipped through hers.

"Am I late?"

"Five minutes."

The rhythm of her steps changed and began to move in harmony with the man's.

"Did your parents say anything?"

Breathing more easily now, she asked:

"What's the film?"

"I don't know. I don't really care. . . ."

They entered the bright lights of a movie house. Lulu's companion left her standing alone in the middle of the lobby while he queued at the box office.

In her kitchen, with the cat installed in the wicker armchair, Laurence was still sitting at the table, slowly eating and reading the newspaper spread out in front of her. Every now and then, she raised her head and listened. She had left the door ajar. Noises came from upstairs, but it was almost impossible to identify them. There were all sorts of things in the

8

attic: crates, an iron bedstead, the children's old cot and high-chair, even a few relics the photographer had left behind. Now, it sounded as though Charles had taken it into his head to clean up the mess. Wasn't that the cabinet he was struggling to move—the big cabinet it had taken four men a great deal of trouble to get up the stairs?

Laurence smiled. She could not help herself. It amused her to imagine her husband wrestling with the furniture.

Camille did not cross Boïeldieu Bridge. On a deserted street, she had slipped into a dark doorway, crossed a damp, badly paved courtyard, and entered a room where a dozen young women were sitting at desks.

This was the shorthand school, this sad, austere class-room lighted by a single naked bulb hanging from the ceiling.

"Please sit down, Mademoiselle Dupeux."

A tall young man was walking between the desks, dictating from an exercise book.

"For your benefit, I'll start again. Are you ready? . . . What was that?"

Her cheeks flushing nearly purple, she repeated in a hoarse voice:

"The lead in my pencil's broken. . . . I'm sorry."

"We'll wait until Mademoiselle Dupeux is ready. . . . I assume you've got a penknife?"

She did not have time to take off her green coat, and she was sure to be too hot, because she sat down right next to the cast-iron stove.

As for Mauricette, she did not go far. Only to the corner. Reaching it, she frowned. Then she waited, annoyed, for five . . . ten minutes.

"If he isn't here in . . ."

Josse's shop was still lighted, as was the one farther down the street, the grocer's which doubled as a greengrocer's. The grade-crossing gate opened for a line of cars; she could see the pale faces of the occupants. The streetcar was waiting to leave.

At last! She took a few steps to the edge of the curb as a large car drew up. A hand reached over. She stooped and got in.

"I'm sorry. I couldn't get away from my wife. . . . Are you angry?"

"Will you drop me in Place du Vieux-Marché first? I've got an errand at my uncle's."

The car moved off and crossed the bridge; a hand stroked Mauricette's knee.

"Will you be long?"

"Your turn to wait!" she replied, jumping out.

As she did so, she looked up and saw light behind the curtains on the second floor, a sort of orange light, which had always, for some reason, struck her as particularly distinguished.

There were three doors: the one to the shop, then the carriage entrance leading to the courtyard, and finally the door of the house, light oak with brass ornaments.

Her uncle, Henri Dionnet, had had to buy three houses on the corner of Rue aux Chaux and demolish them to make way for this, the biggest wholesale grocery in Rouen.

The doorbell chimed. A maid came from a long way away to open the door.

"Oh, it's you, Mademoiselle Mauricette," she said.

Mauricette noticed at once that she was in her best uniform, with a headband and a starched collar.

"Have you got company?"

"Friends of Mademoiselle. But you can go up. . . ."

The whole house smelled of coffee and cinnamon, especially cinnamon.

"Is my uncle here?"

"He's in the living room."

"Tell him I'd like to speak to him."

"Won't you go in?"

No! Because, first, they might keep her, and the car was waiting downstairs. Second, because she would be out of place. She waited in an unlighted doorway. Music and laughter filtered out through a half-open door, along with some of that orange light peculiar to the Dionnets' living room.

Uncle Henri soon appeared. He was a squat man and had a little goatee that looked as rigid and shiny as tin.

"What is it, Mauricette?"

"Mother sent me to ask if there was anything the matter with Father today."

He smelled of cigars and alcohol. His cheeks were pink, as they always were when he had eaten too much. He was wearing his black tie and his stiff shirt front with gold buttons.

"What sort of thing?"

Charles Dupeux was his brother-in-law's bookkeeper.

"I don't know. He came home this evening carrying a lot of packages, went straight upstairs, and locked himself in the attic. He slid a note under the door saying he didn't want to be disturbed. Mother thought . . ."

Henri Dionnet's manner changed. His face all at once took on a cold, businesslike expression.

What had his sister-in-law thought? Obviously that he had provoked Charles! They were always so touchy. As if he hadn't already done enough, giving him a job, out of charity.

"There was nothing the matter with your father."

"That's all right, then."

"Won't you come in for a moment?"

She knew he did not really want her to.

"No, thank you."

"Tell your mother I don't know what's going on. . . . Will you see yourself out?"

Downstairs, two gloved hands tapped against the wheel. Then a hand opened the car door.

11

"Shall we go to Le Havre for a bite to eat? I hear there's this new night club . . ."

The car drove off, plunging into the darkness beyond town, its headlights picking out the rows of trees beside the road.

Laurence waited until it was time to go to bed: she was too fat and heavy to climb the stairs for no reason. She turned out the lights, except for the one in the hall, paused to catch her breath on the second floor, and crept up to the next landing.

"Are you there, Charles? . . . Don't play the fool! I know you're in there. . . . If you're trying to scare me . . ."

She was, in fact, somewhat scared, and could not keep from giving herself away.

"You know, there's quite a difference between you and Uncle Guillaume. . . ."

She listened, but heard nothing. It had happened almost the same way with Uncle Guillaume, but in the country, on a farm near Bréauté. He had returned one evening from the horse market, had unharnessed the mare and fed her her oats, and had put the cart back in its place. Through the small square windowpanes of the farmhouse the family saw him moving about like a ghost in the darkness of the yard. Grandmother poured the soup into the tureen, but nobody was served: in those days, nobody would have dared to eat before the master of the house was ready to. But the children were already nibbling impatiently at their pieces of bread.

"What's he doing?" Guillaume's wife, Elise, had asked. "It hasn't been raining."

If it had rained, he might be taking longer to rub down the mare.

"Go and have a look," Grandmother told the youngest boy.

He went, and ran back crying:

"Papa . . . Papa . . ."

While they had been waiting around the steaming soup tureen, Guillaume hanged himself in the stall next to the mare, who was still munching her oats. Nobody knew why. They thought at first it might be a question of money. Not at all! It was because he had made a girl pregnant, a fifteen-year-old who worked at an inn in Bréauté, and she had died trying to get rid of the child.

If he had not hanged himself, he would have gone to prison. Two years at the most, a lawyer assured them.

And now Laurence was listening for the slightest sound.

"It's no use trying to scare me. . . . I can hear you moving around in there. . . . Have you gone mad? Is that it? . . . Charles!"

She was talking to herself and laughing, trying to keep up her courage.

"Of course, I've always known you weren't like other men. But if it's your idea of fun to play dead . . ."

She had not meant to say the word. She touched wood.

"Are you really going on with this? . . . Well, if that's what you want . . . You'll come out soon enough when you're hungry."

Light showed under the door. But it was no use looking through the keyhole, even though it was quite large, because there was something blocking it. When she shook the door, she felt a resistance, and it occurred to her that her husband had dragged the big cabinet in front of it.

"Well, never mind . . . Good night . . . I hope you enjoy yourself."

She went down to her room and took off her clothes with a sigh of relief, especially her belt, which left marks on her stomach. For once, she was going to have the whole bed to herself. Yet she did not fall asleep right away. She lay looking up at the ceiling, where the street lamp and an arc light from the railway cast reflections through the curtains. And she shouted up:

"Well, Charles? . . . Have you made up your mind? . . . Don't be a child!"

Thoughts raced through her mind, getting ever more confused. Then she heard the front door opening and the creaking of the coatrack in the hall.

"Are you asleep, Mama?"

It was Camille outside the door.

"No."

"Is he still up there?"

Camille came in, but did not switch on the light.

"Can you still hear him?"

"Oh, yes. He moves around sometimes. If he's sleeping on the floor, I wish him luck."

"Good night."

"Good night, Camille."

What she did not know—though it would not have bothered her—was that the shorthand teacher had just seen Camille home.

"You were hard on me again this evening. . . ."

"Don't you understand I do it on purpose?"

Laurence was still only half asleep when Lulu got back. But Lulu did not go into her mother's bedroom. Instead, she listened at all the doors, as if to check whether she was the last one back. Then she took off her shoes and went up to the top floor.

"Papa," she whispered.

There was a slight movement, but no reply.

"Are you asleep?" Lulu asked Camille as she entered the bedroom they shared.

"Yes . . ."

"Is Mauricette back?"

14

"Not yet."

"She's going too far! Did you know he's married? I told her if it went on, I'd tell Papa."

"Let me sleep."

And Camille soon fell asleep again. It seemed to her she'd slept for a long time, when she woke up suddenly and saw her sister, sitting on her bed, looking at her stomach.

"What are you doing?"

"Nothing."

"Then go to sleep."

The trains kept up their noise: they seemed to be at their most strident at night, and there was a constant harsh blowing of whistles, spitting of steam, and grinding of brakes.

"Camille . . ."

Too late! Camille, who had her mother's pale skin and would grow fat and placid like her, lay huddled and moist, fast asleep.

Lulu could not sleep. She watched the rays of light on the ceiling. She heard a car stop on the other side of the grade crossing, a door slam, rapid footsteps, and finally the key in the lock.

All the daughters were back now—except for Marie, the eldest, who had left home two years before. Mauricette took off her shoes downstairs, and opened her door without a sound.

"Mauricette!"

"Shh . . ."

"What time is it?"

"Why do you want to know?"

The door was always open between the two bedrooms.

"I can't hear anything upstairs. . . ."

But at that moment there was a slight noise on the attic floor.

"Go to sleep!" ordered Mauricette.

"What about you?"

15

"Be quiet!"

Camille turned over in bed, and the two girls fell silent. Time passed. Mauricette was alone in the room she had once shared with Marie. The street was again deserted. In the distance, smoke rose from the factory chimneys. The trains . . .

Lulu turned over heavily and lifted her head from the pillow. She had distinctly heard the sound of running water.

"Mauricette!" she whispered.

"What?"

"What are you doing?"

But Camille's thick voice interrupted them:

"Will the two of you please let me sleep?"

Chapter 2

"WHAT DOES HE SAY?"

"Nothing . . . He won't speak. . . . Every now and then he makes a growling sound, like a dog you try to take a bone from."

The movement of Céline's iron set the rhythm for the conversation. Laurence could have stayed here for hours, by the stove, watching Céline work. Céline, with her five children, was always washing or ironing. The two boys were at school. The girl they'd nicknamed the Slug was in kindergarten. The other one was on the floor, in a playpen of turned wood, and the baby was asleep in his cradle.

Through the steamed-up windows it was just possible to make out the yard, cluttered with ladders. Céline's husband, Bobinec, was a painter and decorator. He had once had as many as ten men working under him, but there was only one now. The two of them had left together for a wallpapering job in the neighborhood.

They lived not far from Laurence, at the back of a yard. There was actually a shop in front, with a few rolls of paper and brushes balanced on pots of enamel in the window, but a sign read: ALL INQUIRIES AT THE BACK.

"Hadn't you noticed anything recently?" asked Céline,

17

who was keeping her eye on everything—her ironing, the fire, the child in the pen, and the one in the cradle—as well as occasionally wiping the steam from a windowpane and looking out to see if the vegetable seller had appeared.

Calmly, Laurence continued:

"You know what Charles is like. . . . He comes in, changes his jacket, and sits down to eat. No sooner has he finished than he starts to read the paper, and he doesn't look up again until he asks if it's time to go to bed."

Quite the opposite of Bobinec, who, as Céline said, was exhausting to live with, always moving around, talking, gesticulating, making faces, so that the only time anyone could breathe easily was when he wasn't there.

Céline was the youngest of the Babin sisters. There were three of them—Laurence, the eldest, then Elise, who had married Dionnet, and finally Céline—plus two brothers, Paul and Arthur.

"Isn't it the day for Mama?" asked Laurence.

"Yes. I'm expecting her."

Their mother was alive, a shriveled little old woman, but still strong and alert. She lived alone in one room, but spent one day of the week with each of her children. At Laurence's house, which was always in a mess, she was the one who tidied up. At Céline's, she would grab an iron as soon as she arrived. It was impossible for her to sit still, like Laurence, and let the conversation glide slowly by, with gaps and pauses that made the slow passing of time all the more obvious.

"I tried everything to get through to him. Believe it or not, I was almost afraid to be alone with him in the house. . . . The girls had gone out. . . . Lulu had tried again to make him talk, and had come down in tears. . . . You know her and her father. . . . Anyway, I put my stew in the oven and went upstairs. I was out of breath. . . . I said to him:

" 'I hope you're not going to keep on playing the fool?'

"You have no idea what a strange feeling it is when you know someone's there behind a door but he won't answer you. . . . Occasionally you hear a noise and you wonder what he's doing. . . . Then it's quiet, and you start to shake. . . .

" 'Come on, Charles,' I said again. 'Don't tell me you've gone mad. . . . Or if you have, just say so, and we'll take good care of you.'

"He started walking about. It was infuriating.

" 'Don't you realize what people will think?' I said. 'Not to mention the fact that Henri will be livid if you don't turn up at the office.' "

It was hard to tell if Céline was listening. She looked at her sister from time to time, but there was no flicker of interest on her face, and the proof that she was thinking of something else was that she suddenly opened the door. She had heard the vegetable seller's horn. When she returned, Laurence continued, perfectly naturally:

"I think I'll go and ask Paul what he thinks."

Paul was the elder of their two brothers. He wore a beard and worked for a newspaper as a proofreader.

"He'll be in bed," said Céline.

"His gallstones again? . . . But I can't just do nothing. . . . If anything happened, I'd never be able to forgive myself."

"Why don't you ask Henri?"

"Mauricette went there last night. He claims there's nothing wrong between him and Charles. . . ."

It was ten o'clock. The weather was clear. On the other side of the Seine, Lulu was cleaning the windows of the shoeshop, her body held tightly in a black apron, over which she wore a wide belt like a schoolgirl's.

On the same street, at the corset-maker's, Camille was working with four other girls in a room whose frosted-glass windows let in a chill light.

"You can't work if you're always looking out the windows," the old maid who ran the place would declare.

As for Mauricette, she was typing in an insurance office. She was taking her time, looking around, occasionally stopping to pull a candy from a bag or to buff her nails. She was alone except for a young clerk, who was constantly stealing admiring glances at her.

Their boss did not arrive until ten. He entered the adjoining office, took off his hat, coat, and gloves, smoothed his hair in front of the mirror, and finally opened the door part way.

"Mademoiselle Mauricette!"

She stood up, picked up the mail, and went to take it in to him. The clerk watched her shapely behind as she moved: she had the best figure of the Dupeux girls. She stepped through the door and closed it behind her. A slight smile was hovering on her boss's lips.

"Did your parents say anything?" he asked in a low voice.

His eyes were laughing. He had a greedy but satisfied look on his face.

"No, nothing."

"And tonight?"

She batted her eyelids and then, without transition, said:

"The answer's arrived from England. . . . Lloyd's is refusing the certificate. They say they won't pay unless it's proved that . . ."

Laurence would have to stand up sooner or later. She was still talking a little, to cheer herself up. She talked about Paul, who had such bad luck with his health, and about Arthur, who had changed jobs again and was now a cashier in a movie house.

"I think I'll go to Henri's just the same. . . ."

"Won't you have something to drink?" asked Céline, out of politeness.

20

"No, thanks."

She was on her feet. She was about to leave. She was holding the doorknob.

"Have you had him vaccinated?"

"The doctor's coming next week."

At last! She was in the street, carrying her shopping bag. It was a real string bag, not one of those oilcloth bags most housewives had. Charles had made it himself. He had made one for Céline, too. He was good with his hands. He would often spend all of Sunday alone in a corner working on little jobs of that kind, or else he would stay in the spare room, which he had transformed into a darkroom, developing photographs and printing them with meticulous care, in blue, green, or sepia, using rare types of paper and playing with effects of light and color.

Laurence went past the shoeshop, where Lulu was on her knees in the window. She knocked on the glass to say hello to her, and was reminded that she would need to buy a new pair of slippers one of these days, because her blue ones were worn out.

At the Dionnets', she would try to avoid Henri, who didn't like her, and see her sister. Provided . . .

What was it Henri had said to her the last time, in that ice-cold voice of his, which made his words sound so disagreeable?

"I'd prefer it if you didn't come here without a hat!"

Well, she wasn't wearing a hat this time either. She thought it was ludicrous to put one on just to go shopping. Why not gloves as well, like the judge's wife, who forced her maid to walk behind her with the baskets?

A wagon was just driving in through the carriage entrance. Dionnet had three of them, and six big horses, which he kept in a stable at the far end of the courtyard. The courtyard itself looked like a railway station, with platforms always over-

21

flowing with barrels, bales, and large bottles encased in wicker-work. Laurence entered the shop, as if to buy something; it didn't sell retail to strangers, but the family were allowed to shop there.

She did not speak to the assistant, but waited until Mademoiselle Thérèse, who had been there for twenty years, was free.

"Let me have some split peas and four pounds of flour. . . . Have you still got those canned tomatoes you had last time? . . . "

The shop was huge and thriving: shelves right up to the ceiling, full of the finest canned goods, and counters at least nine yards long, with gleaming scales, big rolls of gray paper, and hanging balls of string.

"Is my sister upstairs?"

Thérèse nodded.

"*All right?*" asked Laurence, giving the words a meaning only the two of them knew.

Thérèse pursed her lips in a way that indicated things weren't exactly all right. Laurence sighed:

"Do you think I can go up? Is he in his office?"

She went through a low door. At the end of a cluttered hallway, a spiral staircase led to the rooms in the house. The kitchen was full of steam.

"Is my sister here?"

"Madame is in her room."

Too bad! It was starting all over again! Who did Elise get it from? Not from her mother, who drank only water. Nor from her father—the brother of the Guillaume who had hanged himself—who may have had lots of faults, but not that one.

"Can I come in?"

There was a grunt in reply, and she pushed open the door and entered a very bright room. The bed was in disarray, and in it she saw Elise's unkempt hair, bleary eyes, and tired face.

22

"Oh, it's you," sighed Elise.

Her voice was thick, and she spoke with difficulty. She tried to sit up.

"Have a chair . . . What did he tell you?"

"I haven't seen Henri."

"Do you know what he did? . . . He locked me in again last night. . . . We had guests. . . ."

"I know. . . . Mauricette was here. . . ."

"If you only knew how painful these migraines are! Pass me a capsule . . . Yes, there, on the dressing table . . . They won't even come and ask me if I need anything. They'd all let me die, all of them."

She swallowed her capsule with a little water. Laurence caught a strong whiff of alcohol.

"It's my head. . . . It feels like an iron bar. . . . Are your children all right?"

"They're all right, thanks."

"When I think that that man, who's rolling in money, makes you pay the same for the goods as everybody else . . . And even so, he reproaches me for it. . . . The way he says 'your family,' anyone would think you were all beggars. . . . Oh, my dear, I'd give so much still to be like the rest of you. . . ."

"Come on now, don't cry."

It was bound to happen. On days like these, Elise would always end up whining and bemoaning her lot, going on about how unhappy she was, how good she was, how she would do anything for them.

"Have you ordered something? . . . Tell Thérèse it's for me. I insist! Tell her not to write it in the book. . . . Listen, Laurence, will you do something for me? . . . I need a pick-me-up . . . In the closet at the end of the hall . . . Yes. The key must be on top. Behind the brooms, you'll find some bottles of stout. . . . Bring me one."

She would begin with stout, as a pick-me-up. Later, she

23

would get up and, in one of the many nooks and crannies of the vast house, unearth a bottle of calvados or cognac, or something else strong, and the whole thing would start again.

"Mama's on a binge!" her daughter would announce coldly.

They had to lock her in her room when there were visitors. They hid her shoes to keep her from going out and drinking in one bar or another. Despite this, she had once got out and wandered the streets in her stocking feet.

"Do you think that's going to do you any good?" Laurence protested feebly. She did not dare refuse, though she was afraid of being caught by her brother-in-law.

"You're not going to side with them, are you? . . . Am I good to you, yes or no? . . . Are you, too, going to say I'm a bad woman?"

"Of course not, Elise . . . Calm down . . ."

"A bad woman . . . Why, I'd give you the shirt off my back. . . . I have nothing to call my own. . . ."

"It's all right. I'll go. . . . But what if Henri . . ."

What she feared happened. As she was returning with the bottle of stout, she ran straight into Henri, who was standing in the doorway. He looked at the bottle, took it, and threw it across the room, where it smashed. He did it calmly, without any obvious anger, in the same way as, when one of his staff had done something wrong, he would give him a hard, silent stare and wait for him to get the jitters.

"I came . . ." began Laurence.

Henri locked the door of his wife's room and put the key in his pocket. The two of them stood on the landing.

"What about your husband?" he asked.

"That's precisely why I came. I wanted to ask you . . ."

She could be familiar with him because she did not work for him. Charles, on the other hand, had to address his brother-

24

in-law formally. Henri demanded it. "In an office, being family doesn't count," he had said.

He did not ask his sister-in-law into any of the rooms. They were still standing at the top of the stairs.

"I wanted to ask your advice. . . . Mauricette must have told you what's going on. . . . Since yesterday, he's been locked in the attic, and he won't answer when we talk to him. All the girls have tried. . . ."

"Is he moving around?"

She knew what he was thinking.

"He was walking around like a madman when I left. . . . I thought of calling a locksmith, but I don't know how he'd react. . . . Not to mention the fact that he's moved the big cabinet in front of the door . . . What would you do in my place?"

He had never had any more color than a block of stone, and it was hard to remember the time when his beard was black, and not this cold gray. He would die without changing complexion or expression, with the same lines on his forehead, the same black spots on his nose, and the same bushy eyebrows, almost as thick as mustaches.

He was nervous. His stubby fingers were fiddling with the watch chain lying across his waistcoat.

"He's said nothing at all?"

"Nothing."

"Has he had any bad news about his daughter?"

"I don't think so. . . . If he'd received a letter, I'd have seen it. . . . I was wondering if the two of you had quarreled. . . . Do you think it's possible for someone to go mad all of a sudden? As Céline says, there isn't any way of knowing if it runs in his family."

Charles was the son of a washerwoman, who had died when he was only five, and he had never known his father.

25

His name, Dupeux, was his mother's. He had been brought up in an orphanage.

"What do you think?"

It was clear that Henri was thinking, thinking hard. He looked as though he were driving a plow; his brows were knit, his mouth tight on his cigar, which had gone out.

"Do you think it's serious, Henri?"

Laurence was pretending to be more worried than she really was, to try to take his mind off the business of the bottle of stout. How could he be severe on a woman who had such misfortunes as hers?

"Haven't you noticed anything lately?"

"You know how he is. . . . I was just saying to Céline . . . He's a man who never makes up his mind one way or the other. He's too meek and mild. If he'd been less meek, he'd surely have got somewhere."

"Come on!" said Henri finally, decisively, and started down the stairs.

She followed him without knowing where they were going. He opened the door to his office, which was a sort of glass cage overlooking the courtyard, like the bridge of a ship. Charles's place, next to the locked safe, was empty. Henri took his bowler, his heavy black overcoat, and his umbrella.

"Are you coming to the house?"

"Yes . . . One moment . . ."

He went down to the courtyard to give orders, then came back to get a cigar from a box on the mantelpiece.

"Let's go!"

She wondered if he would take the car, but they set off on foot. She didn't dare get her shopping. She followed him, embarrassed to be without a hat. He did not speak to her. Every now and then he stopped to relight his cigar. All day long he would have a cigar in his mouth, but almost all day

26

the cigar was out, giving off a smell of stale tobacco, which was also the smell of his beard.

He stopped to wait for the streetcar. He got on, and said to his sister-in-law:

"Go and sit down."

He stayed on the rear platform, and she watched him from inside, aware that he was still thinking and that he was bothered about something.

He was certainly the man they talked about most in the family, and not only because he was the wealthiest. They would repeat his remarks, like the one he had made to Paul's five-year-old son when Elise had given him some candy from a box in the shop:

"Give me that, sonny . . . I don't like people to get into the habit of coming here to fill their pockets."

And he had calmly put the candy back in the glass-lidded box.

Once, when they were pitying Paul because of his bad kidneys, Henri, with his cigar in the corner of his mouth as always, had observed:

"If he's ill, there's nothing he can do about it."

And when Arthur, after being out of work for two months, had tried to borrow money from him, he had refused point-blank.

"Nobody's rich enough to give money to all the people who need it. So it's no use even starting. Besides, you do people a disservice that way."

Although he had not arrived in Rouen in clogs, that wasn't far from the truth. He rarely spoke about his family, but it was known that his father had been a quarryman and that his brother still worked as a stonemason somewhere in the countryside. He had kept the accounts for a grocer. Then he had got to know Bonduel—*how* was a mystery.

Bonduel came from a good family and had inherited some money. His poor health forced him to spend part of the year in the mountains. Until they met, he had lived on his private means.

How had Henri persuaded him to join in starting the Dionnet and Bonduel grocery business?

Nobody remembered much about Bonduel: a very tall young man with pink cheeks, always smartly dressed in pale colors. On the stroke of noon, he would arrive to make a tour of inspection in the warehouses, and then he would go have his port at the Café de la Comédie.

It was said that he had died of overindulgence. Further details were whispered about when the children weren't around: hints that he hadn't been satisfied with the elegant women he was seen with, that he had spent his nights in places of ill-repute, with Dionnet for company. . . .

Laurence remembered the funeral. All the family had gone, and the men stayed afterward for dinner. The week after, Bonduel's name disappeared from the front of the shop. In order not to waste the stock of letterhead and invoices, the name was crossed out in red, and the paper was used for several more years.

Laurence gave a start. They had reached the grade crossing. The motorman was already getting off to prepare for the return trip.

She followed Henri through the crossing gates, which, miraculously, were open. A ray of sunlight broke through fluffy clouds.

"I hope I haven't forgotten my key," she said.

She hadn't forgotten it. The house smelled of something burning. It was the stew, which was now stuck to the bottom of the pot.

"Go on, Henri . . . I'll be right up," she shouted from the kitchen.

He was already on the stairs, going up slowly and heavily. Some of the steps creaked. The staircase seemed too narrow and too flimsy for him. An open door gave him a glimpse of a room in disorder.

He finally stopped climbing.

"Are you there, Charles?" he asked, in his boss's voice.

Silence. Laurence had come to the foot of the stairs and stood with her head raised, listening.

"Can you hear me? . . . Do you plan to continue this prank much longer?"

"Is he moving around?" asked Laurence, from downstairs.

Henri did not reply. He shook the door.

"Do you know what I'm going to do, Charles? I'm going to the police station and bring back a policeman and a locksmith. . . . Then we'll see what this is all about."

There were footsteps. Laurence heard them from downstairs. But the door still did not open.

Henri pretended to walk downstairs, to carry out his threat. He slowly descended four or five steps, then turned. At that moment, a piece of paper appeared under the door, as if with a life of its own.

Henri went back up and bent down. Laurence was still listening. She heard her brother-in-law coming down. His step was no longer hesitant. When he appeared, he seemed harder than ever.

"Well?"

He stopped and looked at the narrow hall, at the door to the living room, but decided to head for the glass door to the kitchen. Still wearing his overcoat and with his bowler on his head, he sat down in the wicker armchair; the cat jumped off just in time.

"Has he written something again?"

She hardly dared ask him for the piece of paper. He was

29

looking at it with absent eyes. Finally, with a sigh, as if loath to part with it, he held it out to her.

Charles had written, in pencil:

If you don't leave me in peace, I'll shoot. And that's just the beginning!

"What does he mean?"

Henri did not react, merely continued to stare at the tips of his shoes. Laurence went into the next room. It was neither a dining room nor a living room. There was a sideboard and an oak table with a runner and two empty vases on it, but there was also a harmonium and a sewing machine, a chaise longue and a small mahogany pedestal table.

Nobody in the house ever played the harmonium. Charles had bought it at an auction, though he could not read a note of music. All one Sunday he had tried out hymn tunes, jerkily pressing the pedals and producing quavery sounds. Since then, nobody had opened the lid. Old newspapers were piled on top of it.

Near the window facing the street was another piece of furniture that had been bought at an auction: Charles's roll-top desk.

They had never had a key for it. Laurence lifted the cover and pulled open a drawer.

"It's true!" she said. "The revolver's gone. . . . I wonder if it works. . . . I don't even know if there were any bullets. . . ."

She was surprised to see Henri standing behind her. She had not heard him approach, and she had raised her voice, thinking he was still in the wicker armchair in the kitchen.

"Do you think he'd kill himself?" she asked.

He did not reply, and she was more and more surprised. She could feel him close to her, smelling of stale cigar. He leaned over and opened drawers, one after the other. Then, without saying a word, he pulled up a chair, sat down, and placed his elbows on the desk.

"What are you thinking?"

His silence overawed her. She watched him open bottles of colored ink, one after the other.

"Why don't you answer me? . . . Do you really think he'd do himself harm?"

The oppressive atmosphere came not so much from Charles, locked in his attic, as from this man in an overcoat, who seemed about to crush the yellow desk with his weight. Why didn't he say anything? Why was there something shifty in his look, which was usually so set?

"What's the matter, Henri? Have you discovered something new?"

"What?" he grunted, looking at her suddenly, as if surprised to see her so near.

"I said . . ."

Drama was not her style. She very quickly saw the funny side of things.

"What a face you're making!"

"Listen, Laurence . . ."

"I'm listening. . . ."

"I think your husband . . ."

He stopped and frowned.

"Is it so difficult to come out with it?"

"Be quiet . . . Try to be serious, for once in your life . . . I think it's better to leave him alone. . . . He'll eventually calm down, by himself. . . . The less we bother him, the better it will be."

He did not stand up. He stayed there at the little desk—secondhand, like most of the furniture in the house.

"But what's he going to eat?" objected Laurence. Then, after a few moments' thought: "Maybe those packages?"

She almost burst into nervous laughter. It was too funny! Had he really taken the precaution of stocking provisions?

One thought led to another. He not only needed to eat;

he needed to drink. And she suddenly went into the kitchen, where the only water tap in the house was. She looked under the sink.

"He's been down!" she cried triumphantly. "He took advantage of my going out. . . . The jug's gone. . . . He must have filled it with water and taken it up."

She hesitated to laugh, no longer knowing whether it was funny or serious. Another thought occurred to her: he not only needed to eat and drink; there were other bodily needs. . . . What about . . . ?

"Listen, Henri, I think . . ."

What was she about to say? That the whole thing was a farce? She did not finish, because just then Henri stood up, looking as solemn as if he were at a funeral, carefully buttoned his overcoat, and looked around for his umbrella.

"I've given you my advice. You can do whatever you wish, but if I were in your shoes, I'd just leave him alone."

It was serious, then. For a man like Dionnet to be so affected by it . . . All at once, the house seemed different to her, and again she was almost afraid to stay there alone.

"Can I offer you anything? . . . A drop of port?"

"Nothing, thanks. I'll go now."

He was in the hall, blocking it completely.

"You haven't told me what you were thinking. . . . What if I go see a doctor?"

"What good would that do?"

He opened the door and went straight out, barely turning to say good-bye to her. Laurence stood in the doorway watching him walk away and cross the railroad tracks. Madame Josse was on the doorstep of her shop.

"Is someone ill?" she asked.

Why did she ask that? Oh, yes, of course! Henri never came to the house. The neighbors did not know him. Madame

Josse had seen his black coat, bowler, and umbrella and had taken him for a doctor.

"No one, Madame Josse."

"You know, if you want some black pudding, we killed a pig this morning."

"Thank you . . . I'll come by later."

She closed the door, and was struck by the emptiness of the house, so much so that she gave a start when the cat, jumping into the armchair, made the wickerwork squeak.

As she passed the stairs, she could not help looking up and murmuring, as if to reassure herself:

"He's clever!"

Then she wondered what she was going to make for dinner instead of the burned stew.

Chapter 3

IT WAS CAMILLE WHO WENT TO THE DOOR WHENEVER ANYONE rang or, more often, knocked on the mailbox. She was always the one who did the work, whether it was wiping the dishes, darning the stockings, or going down to the cellar; by the time she was twelve, people had already started saying that she was like a little mother.

An extremely rare thing had happened that Sunday. Laurence had lost her temper.

"I'd like to see you try to go out on a day like today, when . . ."

A day when what? She had searched for an end to the sentence. It was not quite right to say that they had had a misfortune, because nothing really bad had happened yet. Nor that there was a sick person in the house, because they didn't know if that was so.

". . . well, a day like today!" she had concluded.

What had impressed her was not so much Charles in his attic as the fact that Henri Dionnet, who was not easily affected by anything, had taken the streetcar with her, gone upstairs, examined the desk, and, far from shrugging it off, had seemed worried.

Mauricette had locked herself in her room. If she couldn't go out, she would at least avoid a boring family gathering.

Downstairs, Camille opened and closed the door. As for Lulu, she had said nothing. Nobody had taken any notice of her, and she must have seized the opportunity to escape, since she was nowhere to be seen in the house.

"Haven't you brought the children?" Laurence asked Céline. Bobinec was with her, wearing a checked suit and extraordinary yellow shoes.

"I asked Mama to come and look after them. They're so unruly. . . ."

And she looked up at the ceiling. It was her equivalent of "a day like today."

She had the baby with her, however, because he was still breast-feeding. They made up a sort of nest for him on the sofa, and he fell asleep. A little later, Paul nearly sat down on him, but a cry from Céline stopped him in time.

Paul had come, despite his kidneys, or his bladder. Nobody had ever been quite sure which of the two he suffered from, probably both, as well as from something else he preferred not to talk about, for which he was always having injections.

It was rare for a Sunday to go by without two or three of the families, usually with all the children, coming to the Dupeux house, and not only because Laurence was the eldest sister. The large kitchen, with its glass roof, its oleanders, and its disorder, had a lot to do with it. Quite a number of people could fit in, especially because the door to the front room was a folding one. And since disorder was the rule, everyone could do whatever they liked.

On the way to get chairs from the second floor, Camille tried to open Mauricette's door.

"Are you asleep?"

"No."

"Aren't you coming down?"

"No."

35

"What are you doing?"

"Nothing."

She was lying on her bed reading. It didn't bother her that she had to stay in. She couldn't see *him* on Sundays, and she never knew what to do with herself; she didn't like going to the movies on a day when the theater was crowded.

He was a count, a real one, the Comte de Veillet, but since he had become an insurance broker, he had stopped putting his title on his visiting card. His wife had a little money, and for her dowry her father had built them a villa high on a hill overlooking the Dieppe road. They already had a girl of ten and two little boys, and were expecting another child.

It was strange for a man like him. It was hard to imagine him spending Sundays with his family, especially with his parents-in-law, who were decent but rather vulgar people.

Mauricette did not need to move from her bed to know what was going on now. She recognized the footsteps and voices in the hall. It was the same each time, a kiss on the left cheek, a kiss on the right.

"Hello, Auntie . . ."

"Hello, Céline . . ."

"Where are your children?"

"Mama's looking after them."

A glance at the ceiling.

"Still nothing new?"

"He took the bread that Lulu left on the landing. . . . We didn't hear him; so he must have waited until there was no one in the house."

"That shows he doesn't want to do himself any harm!"

"Have you had your coffee?"

"Thanks. We've just eaten."

"Camille! Mathilde will have a cup of coffee."

The two brothers, Paul and Arthur, were smoking, as was Bobinec; already a bluish cloud hung above everyone's head.

36

Although it would have been hard to say why, it was obvious that this gathering was out of the ordinary; it was rather like the evening after a funeral, when the family stays together for a few more hours.

Between his yellow teeth, Paul held a long curved pipe, which he had burrowed into so much that the wood had lost its thickness. He was well aware that he was the head of the family; that was clear from the way he tilted his chair back and looked at everyone with his crafty little eyes.

People in the street often took him for an artist, or else a pastor or a rabbi, because of his black beard, his overlong and always loose-fitting clothes, and his wide-brimmed hat.

His wife, Mathilde, was pale and retiring. Their daughter, Berthe, who was also studying shorthand, had brought her notebook to work on in a corner.

"Shall we do some exercises later on?" she had asked Camille.

"If I have time . . ."

Her face was constantly covered with eczema or pimples, and to hide them she added a layer of cream and powder, which formed a sort of plaster.

"How many days has he been up there now?" asked Bobinec, in his sonorous voice.

"Almost three including today."

Paul said nothing and took little puffs on his pipe, knowing that his hour would come, knowing that he was the one they all expected something from. He was the brains. At any rate, he was a man without prejudices.

The proof was that he had a second family, with another daughter, almost the same age as Berthe, and that he made no secret of the fact. Moreover, he was not even legally married to Mathilde. He had given her due warning:

"I consider marriage a folly and a trap. Man has the right to live as he pleases. I'm free, and so are you. I won't ask you

37

to account for your actions, and I'll never account to you for mine. . . ."

It could not have been clearer. He made sure that everyone knew it. His other wife was a former singer. She was always heavily made up and dressed as if for a carnival, though she was apparently a very serious person.

"What does everyone want to eat at four o'clock?" Laurence asked.

"We aren't hungry. . . ."

"But you'll be hungry soon. The girls'll go to the pastry shop. Camille and Berthe, go and get some brioches and some Genoa cake. . . . And get a bottle of vermouth for Paul at the same time. My purse is in the drawer. . . ."

Céline asked:

"What did Henri say?"

"He advised me to leave him alone. . . . Paul, you know about these things. . . . I don't know exactly what happened. . . . He rummaged through the desk. I got the feeling something upset him, but I had a look afterward and couldn't see anything. . . ."

The day was waning. Above their heads, above the cloud of smoke, the glass roof was like a piece of pearl-gray material, but they always waited until the last moment to switch the light on, because the semidarkness made for a cozier feeling.

"By and large," said Arthur, who was virtually the image of Paul, without a beard but in equally bad health, "by and large, he's never been ill."

Laurence called Paul to witness.

"You remember, Paul! I told you about it five or six years ago. . . . He was getting so thin I thought he might have TB, and I persuaded him to see a doctor. It turned out to be tapeworm. . . ."

Bobinec had sat down at the harmonium and was drawing comical sounds from it. Paul frowned. All the Babins loathed

Bobinec, who was too loud and who played comedy roles in an amateur dramatic society.

"I thought he might have had news of Marie," said Céline, "but Laurence says no. . . ."

"If Marie had written, I'd have known. I always empty the mailbox when I come down."

"Does anyone know what's become of her?"

"She's on the street, that's what!" sneered Bobinec.

"Can't you be quiet?"

"Why? What's the matter? She was seen, wasn't she? You know as well as I do. The time before last that Girodin was in Paris . . ."

"She's doing what she wants, and it's none of our business," said Paul conclusively. "We each of us do what we want, even playing the clown if that's all we're capable of. . . ."

"That's telling him!"

It would end in a quarrel, as always happened when the brothers-in-law met.

"Why don't we set the table?" suggested Laurence, to change the subject.

The only one of the Babin sons and daughters missing was Elise.

"Have you seen her? How was she?"

"In the middle of a binge . . . I was caught by Henri as I was getting her a bottle of stout from the closet. . . ."

"Do you think our father . . . ?"

"I'm sure our father didn't drink!" declared Paul. "I knew him better than any of you."

It was strange how all at once the atmosphere changed.

"I went with him to Düsseldorf, that time he was selling cider. . . ."

"It's funny," remarked Bobinec. "It seems he was a big, strong man, yet it's his daughters who are big and strong, while his sons . . ."

Céline gestured to him to be quiet, and he shrugged.

"One day when he was angry," said Paul, "I saw him take two men by the scruff of the neck and knock their heads together until they collapsed like rag dolls."

"Do you have a picture of him, Céline?"

"A small one, but it's quite faded. He was already ill when it was taken."

"Does anyone know exactly what he died of?"

"Yes, I know."

It was Paul speaking again. He removed his pipe a little way from his lips. At times, he used the stem of the pipe to smooth his mustache.

"He died of cancer of the intestine."

"Does it run in the family?"

He shrugged. He always gave the impression of knowing things it was pointless to discuss.

"All in all . . ." It was impossible to keep Bobinec quiet, with his *all in all*s. "All in all, he was like Arthur. A jack-of-all-trades and master of none."

"He had so many jobs because he could do everything. . . ."

"And while he stayed away for months, his family got by as best they could."

"He never failed to send us money!" retorted Céline, glaring at her husband. "Anyway, I don't know why we're talking about Papa; it's Charles we should be discussing. . . . What do you think, Paul?"

"I certainly don't think he was happy. . . ."

"Why do you say that?" protested Laurence, hurt.

"Just because!"

The girls returned with the brioches, cake, and vermouth.

"Isn't Lulu here?" asked Mathilde in surprise, as if suddenly waking up.

"Oh, that's right!" said Céline. "We passed her on the way. She was in a hurry, wasn't even wearing a hat. . . . We thought she was running an errand in the neighborhood. . . ."

Camille looked at her mother. Laurence appeared not to have heard. There was no point in making a family drama out of it.

Lulu had not put her hat on because, having left it in the kitchen, she would not have been able to get it without attracting attention. She put on her coat only after passing the grade crossing. And she ran, in fact, for fear of being called back. She turned around several times. Her long, insect-thin legs strode along the dry, echoing sidewalk. A streetcar passed, but she did not manage to catch it.

She knew all the uncles and aunts would be in the house. But she had given her word, and that was quite as important as their discussions and Paul's speeches.

She had given her word! In the darkness of the movie house, Georges had whispered in her ear:

"Sunday?"

She had squeezed his hand. All the blood seemed to have drained out of her. She had said yes.

Then, a long time after, as they were watching the film and his hand was groping beneath her dress, she asked:

"Where?"

"Don't worry . . . A friend of mine will lend me his room."

As she hurried through the empty streets, she turned around, as if both fearing and hoping that someone would come and stop her. Her mind was made up! And so . . .

For a moment, she thought that Georges was not at the meeting place, near Boïeldieu Bridge, but he was hidden by the newsstand. He looked with surprise at her unruly hair and felt her hot, short breath.

"I couldn't put my hat on because . . ."

There was still time. In the gray light, people were entering

41

a movie theater. She and Georges had already seen that particular film, but they could always find another.

Georges was taking her through an area they had never been in before.

"Is it far?"

"Right near here."

He was wearing new shoes and had put eau de cologne on his hair.

"Don't you think . . . ?"

No! What was the point? Her mind was made up. She would have to do it one of these days anyway. . . .

Nevertheless, she drew back a little when they turned into an alleyway that smelled of garbage pails. Georges held her arm and drew her down a passage with a yard at the end of it. But they did not go as far as the yard. On the right was a staircase, which was hard to make out in the dark. A rope served as a handrail.

"Be careful! Follow me."

Her mouth was dry.

"It's nothing. You'll see. . . ."

He had very thick brown hair, growing low on his forehead. He worked in a garage, and all the girls talked about him.

"Have you seen Georges?"

"Don't you see Georges any more?"

"Guess who I saw Georges with!"

He was wearing a tight-fitting new suit, greenish in color, and shoes with square toes.

He announced, without even looking at the room, which he probably knew well:

"My friend won't be back until six. . . ."

Somebody was timidly knocking at the door. For a long time, Mauricette did not reply. She was absorbed in a novel, her eyelids half closed because of her cigarette smoke. She had burned a hole in the counterpane.

"Are you there?"

"Who is it?"

"Berthe . . . I wanted to say hello."

"I can't let you in at the moment. . . ."

That poor idiot Berthe! You could ask her to do anything, and she'd do it.

"I brought you a piece of cake. . . ."

"I'm not hungry."

Berthe went downstairs, put the plate with the piece of cake on the table, and sat down near the stove. Camille had refused to do shorthand exercises with her. Nobody ever wanted to do anything with her. And she did not dare try to follow the conversation around her.

"I'm not saying he had a vice," said Paul, relighting his pipe and tilting his chair.

"Paul!" interrupted Céline, indicating Berthe with her chin.

"My daughter can hear anything. As for Camille, if at the age of twenty she doesn't know what a vice is . . ."

Yet Camille blushed, thinking of her shorthand teacher, who had never even kissed her.

"And when I say vice . . . well, look, here we have a man who was interested in . . . What? . . . Nothing."

"Photography," muttered Laurence.

"That couldn't be enough for a man who was quite well educated. . . ."

Wasn't it strange to be talking about Charles in the past tense, as if he were dead? Laurence, who was not usually sensitive, was struck by this, and for a few seconds she felt an involuntary desire to cry. It was true that the lights had not been switched on yet, and a gloomy twilight was invading the kitchen, like ashen dust.

"It can't have been much fun for him at Dionnet's. . . . To be quite honest, I'd never have accepted a post like that. . . ."

"It was the only one he could find."

"He wasn't interested in politics. He didn't play the clown, like Bobinec. . . ."

The funny thing was that this was true. For five days, Céline had had to spend every evening sewing together, to Bobinec's specifications, an amazing costume for him to sing comic songs in.

"So I say there was something else. . . ."

"Would you like to have a look in his desk?"

Paul let himself be persuaded, shrugged condescendingly, and went into the living room. That was when he almost sat on Céline's baby.

Céline took the opportunity to feed the baby. The lights were switched on.

"What did Henri look at in particular?"

"I don't know. . . . Everything, really."

Sitting at the desk, Paul, with his beard, with his yellow complexion, his little eyes, his black clothes, looked like a virtuoso forced by enthusiastic music lovers to sit down and play on a badly tuned piano.

He was ten years older than the eldest of the sisters and fifteen years older than his brother, Arthur. Their mother had been barely twenty when he was born. He was the only one of them who knew that she was not married at the time, or, rather, that the wedding had taken place just five months before the birth. It was the period when his father owned a big farm. He could remember it. He could even remember the day everything was sold, a rainy autumn day, with crowds coming from miles around, all the contents of the house spread out in the open air, people opening drawers and examining objects.

Laurence had been born in Paris, where their father was

a coachman, though she did not know this; in the family, it was said that he "worked with horses."

Then came Lille, where Babin had been a foreman in a textile mill.

Had he really been a foreman? He didn't even know the trade. Probably an ordinary worker, maybe even an unskilled laborer. What did it matter?

"What did he do with all these inks?" asked Paul, putting on the steel-rimmed glasses he wore at the newspaper.

Laurence had no idea. Why should she have troubled herself with what Charles did for hours on end, as long as he left her in peace?

"I once saw him drawing printed letters," interrupted Camille, who immediately regretted it, wondering if she had said the right thing.

"What letters?"

"I don't know. . . ."

Bobinec had sat down again at the harmonium. His wife's white, fleshy breast hung out of her blouse as she suckled the baby. Laurence restoked the stove.

"If he's having an affair, we certainly won't find any evidence in a desk that can't be locked."

Laurence burst out laughing.

"An affair?"

"Why not?"

"Charles, an affair? . . . My dear Paul! . . . I still wonder how he managed to father four children. . . ."

She laughed bawdily, as if conjuring up precise images. She repeated:

"Poor Charles! . . . An affair? Him?"

He wasn't a man, but a sheep, with wavy fair hair, girlish complexion, thin white hands—hands that everyone admired.

"Charles has an artist's hands. . . ."

An artist! The only art Charles knew anything about was photography.

"Poor Charles . . ."

"He wouldn't be the first. It isn't necessarily a question of physical prowess."

Camille blushed and turned her face to the wall; she was sorry now she had not accepted her cousin's offer to do short-hand exercises. Céline would have liked to stop her brother, because of the girls.

"A man doesn't lock himself in his attic unless he's mad or he's had a shock. . . . I think he's hiding . . . that's the truth of it. . . . And if he's hiding . . ."

Paul had placed his glass of vermouth on the desk. He took a gulp.

"Let's suppose he's done something stupid. . . . What could it be? . . . Maybe he told Henri what he thought of him, what we all think of him."

"Paul!"

"What's the matter? Henri's my brother-in-law and he's rich, but the fact remains, he's a sorry specimen. . . . But if Charles had done that, we'd all know about it. . . . Alternatively, he might have killed someone."

They heard Laurence burst into almost hysterical laughter. The idea of her husband committing a murder . . .

"Paul!" said Céline. "You're going too far."

"Some very respectable people have been murderers. . . . Or maybe he forged Henri's signature . . ."

"Charming family!" muttered Bobinec.

"What?"

"I said, charming family."

"Please," sighed Céline, "don't let's quarrel."

"Don't forget, it was your brother who started this. . . ."

Laurence, who never saw harm in anybody, remarked:

"If Charles had stolen something, I hope he'd have given

46

me the money to pay the gas bill. Only the day before yesterday, they came and threatened to cut us off. . . ."

What was it that drove Camille to steal out of the room, followed by an inquisitive look from her cousin, and creep to the foot of the stairs? Was it the feeling that they were talking about her father as if he were dead, as if he no longer belonged in the world of the living, even though . . .

She stood motionless in the blue-tinged darkness. The light with the colored-glass shade was still off. Upstairs, everything was quiet and calm. Mauricette, who had unfastened her skirt because it was too tight, was still reading and smoking one cigarette after another in the circle of light provided by her bedside lamp.

"All the same, you must have money," remarked Paul, sucking on his pipe.

"If I had money . . ."

"I don't mean you, Laurence. But Charles . . ."

"If he has, he's never told me about it. . . ."

She was skeptical. Paul took another sip of his drink. He was carefully spacing out its effects.

"Unless I'm mistaken, this is a bond coupon, isn't it? . . . What's more, an American bond, which must be worth a lot. . . ."

"Let me see that . . ."

Camille came back in, silently. Her cousin looked at her, still hopeful that she would notice her.

"A coupon, you say?"

"A coupon that should have been cashed in last month . . ."

"Where did you find it?"

"At the bottom of this drawer."

Silence. The pipe sputtered. The stove took the opportunity to roar. There were flies in the sugar bowl and on what was left of the cake. A train whistled—the first time that day that a train had whistled so loudly.

"I can't think what he could have . . ."

The baby was crying. Céline hummed a vague tune, without looking at him.

"It's not possible that . . ."

"Still, this is a coupon, torn from a bond that must be worth at least six thousand francs. . . ."

"Good Lord!" exclaimed Laurence.

She was quite amazed. So Charles . . . She felt like laughing. No, it wasn't possible! Not him!

"Where could he have got it? He earns only twelve hundred francs at Henri's."

Slowly and solemnly, Paul closed the desk and looked around for the nonexistent key.

"It's a fact!"

Now he could take off his glasses, blink, drink his vermouth, and wipe his beard with the stem of his pipe.

"So according to you . . ."

Berthe approached her cousin. She understood nothing of all this business, and she was bored.

"Can we go to your room?"

"Not now."

Paul was the judge, and it was time to pass sentence. He looked at the floor and puffed calmly at his pipe.

Camille was the only one to catch a faint sound from the direction of the front door. It was Lulu, outside in the now dark street, taking off her shoes on the doorstep and carefully inserting her key.

She saw light under the door of the living room and sniffed a strong smell of tobacco, mingled with the sweeter smells of cake and alcohol. She took three big steps. Some of the stairs creaked, so she had to walk up cautiously. She must go straight to her room and wash herself, as she had heard Mauricette doing, and hide part of her underwear.

Had Georges's friend done it on purpose? They were still in bed when they had heard the key turn in the lock. Georges had simply said:

"Come in! We're finished. . . ."

She had almost reached the second-floor landing. She was looking down, not paying attention to her surroundings. Then she raised her head toward the lines of light framing Mauricette's door.

She had the feeling that on her right . . . She peered into the darkness, then stood stock still, her mouth open. For a moment, the figure she had made out did not move. . . .

Her father was as surprised as she was. He was leaning over the banister, as if listening to the voices downstairs. She barely recognized him, because his beard had grown.

She opened her mouth. She had no idea if she would have cried out, but he put his finger to his lips, with an expression she had never seen before on his face. He was her father and, at the same time, the ghost of her father. He was like a creature in a dream, and he seemed to understand things that people only understood in dreams.

He was making her his accomplice. She must not talk, or cry out, or make any noise. He had his secret, just as she did. Like her, he was unhappy. He was an outsider. They were both outsiders!

Shh! . . . He lifted a foot and went up one step, still leaning on the banister.

She had to keep quiet. Her father's eyes were begging her to keep quiet. . . . And, by way of compensation, they contained a mysterious promise.

Shh! . . . There was no need for the others to know. Just the two of them . . . She was breathing heavily, but had not moved.

Promise? . . .

Suddenly, he turned and quickly climbed to the top floor. She heard the metallic noise of the lock, then his footsteps, no longer muffled.

"Is that you?" came Mauricette's slurred voice.

Who did she mean? Lulu did not reply.

"Camille!" Mauricette called again. "Bring me up a piece of cake. . . ."

There were raised voices downstairs. Surely Uncle Paul and Uncle Bobinec, quarreling at last. Céline must be heaving a sigh. She was used to it. She was caught in the crossfire. The family had never been able to accept Bobinec.

Mauricette lifted herself on one elbow and listened, surprised that there had been no reply. All she could hear was a scratching sound, like a mouse. It was Lulu, who had finally entered her room and locked the door, remembering that she had to wash herself quickly and . . .

"Be quiet, Bobinec! Do you hear? If you carry on like this . . ."

It was Céline.

As for Paul, with his smile, his beard, and his head surrounded by a halo of smoke, he looked like a saint in a stained-glass window.

"One day you'll see I'm right. Charles is a man like any other. . . ."

Then, after a pause:

"What if we all go and have something to eat?"

It would have been too much work for Laurence to make dinner for everyone.

Chapter 4

WHEN CAMILLE JOINED HER IN THE STREET, WHICH WAS
shrouded in cold morning fog, Lulu said to her:

"I'm sure you're late, my girl! You'd better take the streetcar."

The streetcar was waiting on the other side of the grade
crossing, its lights on, its windows steamy.

"The reason I waited for you is that I wanted to walk
with you and have a talk," replied Camille.

She was always paler in the morning than during the rest
of the day, her features blurred and her eyes sleepy, but she
was obviously already willing to do whatever was asked of
her, even if she received small thanks for it. She usually left
the house before her sisters, because the corset-maker made
her employees start work at eight in the morning, even though
the lights had to be kept on for a long time due to the dimness
in the room caused by the frosted glass.

"I'm listening, my girl. But I warn you, you're wasting
your time."

As always, Lulu was walking fast, her hands buried in
her coat pockets, her long neck thrust forward, her hair strag-
gling comically from beneath her beret.

Camille, who was plump and, like her mother, had difficulty breathing, found it hard to keep up with her.

"Listen, Lulu . . ."

"What?"

Lulu already knew, or guessed, though she wondered how her sister had found out.

"What did you do yesterday?"

"I went to the movies."

"That's not true."

"All right, it's not true!"

And she strode on, her neck still thrust forward.

"Where did you do it?"

"Do what?"

Perhaps, deep down, Lulu wasn't too annoyed by the conversation? She was barely sixteen. Camille was twenty, nearly twenty-one. Yet Lulu was the one it had happened to! And, despite everything, Camille felt something close to respect and admiration for her.

"Don't walk so fast . . . Listen . . . I found Mauricette's douche. . . ."

"So?"

"It was in your wardrobe, still wet. . . . Who did you do it with?"

"What business is it of yours?"

"Have you thought of what might happen?"

"You're an idiot, my girl. Mauricette's been doing it for more than a year, and has anything happened to her? Is that all you wanted to say to me?"

"You're forgetting you're only sixteen."

"And you're twenty and still waiting. . . . Look, there's a friend of mine from the shop."

They had reached the bridge. Lulu ran forward, shouting.

Camille gave a start. Near her in the crowd of people going to work, a voice asked:

"Is your mother at home?"

It was Uncle Paul, in his big hat and black clothes. He

didn't work the same hours as most people, because of the newspaper's press time. He started near the end of the afternoon and finished late at night, usually having dinner at three in the morning in a little restaurant in the central market. He slept little and claimed not to need much sleep.

Whenever he went to see Laurence, it was nearly always at nine in the morning, when she had not yet washed or dressed.

He almost never went to see the others. At Céline's, there was not only Bobinec, whom he could not stand, but also the children, whose screaming and smells he found equally unpleasant. As for Elise, it was impossible to go see her, because he had quarreled with Dionnet.

He strolled along unhurriedly, smoking his pipe and walking with his toes turned out; he had flat feet. He knocked on the mailbox. When his sister opened the door, he did not say hello but let out an indistinct grunt, walked in as if it were his own home, and headed straight for the kitchen.

This time, he indicated the upper floors with his head, as if to say:

"Still up there?"

And Laurence shrugged, as if to reply:

"Of course! He's sticking to his guns. . . ."

He had never hung his overcoat on the coatrack. He would keep it on until he reached the kitchen, then place it on a chair, sit down without a word, empty his pipe on the floor, fill the other one he always had with him, and finally, if it was cold, as it was today, open the stove and put his feet up on the lowered lid.

Today, Laurence was peeling vegetables for the stockpot. She knew it was better to keep quiet when Paul was around. He could sit there for a quarter of an hour making no other sound than a small wet noise as he sucked on his pipe.

She had often wondered why he came, whether it was out of affection for her or because he did not feel at home in his own house. It was not unusual for him to stand up after half an hour's silence and leave, sighing:

"Good-bye, my girl."

At other times, he would finally stare at the little picture on the wall between the mirror and the calendar. It was an oil painting in dull colors. Paul had done it long ago, when he was young and had ambitions to become a painter. It was strange, really, that, after successive divisions of the family property, it should have ended up at Laurence's, rather than with one of the other children.

The picture showed an orchard in blossom in April, a pond with ducks and geese, and in the background a long white country house, with wisteria around the door and a dog lying on the threshold. It was the house where Paul had been born.

He pulled on his pipe, let out the smoke in little puffs, and made the wickerwork of the armchair creak, which was a sign that he was about to say something.

"Do you know what Mama was when our father married her?"

There was no point in answering him. In reality, he was talking to himself. Perhaps that was why he came to see Laurence: with her he could say whatever he liked, and it didn't matter.

"When Papa got to know Mama, she was a waitress in a café in Le Havre. . . ."

It was always startling to learn such basic facts about the family so casually, in the course of his reflections, and it made everyone wonder how they could have been ignorant of them for so long.

"Are you sure of that?" asked Laurence, surprised. "In a café?"

He was quite impressive at moments like this, narrowing his eyes and sitting there still as a statue. It was easy to understand what Bobinec meant when he said that his brother-in-law was like a rabbi; after all, he was the guardian of the family history, as if it were Biblical truth.

This history obviously bothered him, since he often returned to it, though never in a coherent way. On one occasion, he recalled their stay in a small town in the center of France, where their father had bought a truck in order to collect vegetables from the neighboring villages; at another time, he spoke of their father's departure for Tunisia, where they were supposed to join him as soon as he was settled.

"In a café!" he repeated, with a kind of relish.

He relighted his pipe and stared vacantly at the carrot his sister was grating with her sharp knife.

"Don't you see what that means? . . . I'm sure that's how it all started. . . ."

In point of fact, Laurence did not especially care for these conversations. She could never understand how it was possible to worry about things that were long past, so that, for example, it bored her to learn that her mother had been a waitress. She could have asked:

"How what started?"

Instead, she stood up to turn off the gas and get some potatoes from the entrance to the cellar.

"The Babins were rich. . . . For two generations, they were the richest people in their village. They were mayors, had been from father to son, like lords of the manor. . . . And what happened? . . . Papa's brother hanged himself. . . . Papa married a waitress. . . . Then the rest of us, every one of us . . ."

"What do you mean?"

"You don't seem to understand. . . . For example, what's become of Arthur, despite all his studies? He's tried every kind of job, always common ones, and chosen a wife who's common."

"Do you think Clémence is that common?"

He could have replied:

"Just like you, my girl! Like all of us! It's as if we'd all inherited a taste for the common, a need to be common. . . ."

He had never really thought it out clearly enough to be able to say it. But he had only to look around him. The mere presence of Laurence was enough to create a plebeian atmosphere anywhere, a kind of flabby, free-and-easy atmosphere. And that was precisely what Paul came to wallow in.

It was the same at Céline's. What could be more common than Bobinec? And Arthur lived in a little two-room apartment overlooking a courtyard.

Even Elise had to escape from her house and go and drink in the most sordid bars she could find!

"So, according to you, we get that from Mama?"

That wasn't it either. It was more complicated than that. The mystery was much wider, infinite even, since Paul had been trying for years to get to the bottom of it.

"Why do you think all the daughters in the family are fat?"

"How should I know?"

"It's because of your livers."

"You know very well I've never suffered from my liver! Neither has Céline."

"All the same, both of you are paying for the fact that our grandparents ate and drank too much."

She felt like laughing, as she always did when new vistas were opened to her.

"What an idea!"

"As for Arthur and me, maybe we're paying for other excesses. . . . Do you know how many syphilitics there are in Normandy?"

"You're not saying our father . . ."

He would solve the mystery in the end. Someday, he would succeed in drawing together all the scattered threads, and everything would become clear. He would finally understand why none of them, for all their good intentions, would ever amount to anything, and why, each time they tried to raise themselves, they fell back into the same almost grubby mediocrity.

"You're worrying about things that aren't worth it. Why can't you just take life easy, like anyone else? You've got a good job. . . ."

"I bet you don't even know who your husband's father was. I was thinking about it last night on my way home. I kept on thinking about it in bed. . . . It's possible the solution lies on that side of the family. . . ."

Laurence turned the faucet on and washed the vegetables in an enamel pail. The cat was rubbing against her legs, meowing. She pushed it away.

"Later! Is it my fault the milkman hasn't come yet? . . . What were you saying, Paul? That you know Charles's father?"

"I used to know him, when his mother lived on Rue aux Ours. . . . I was only a child, but I remember her very well, a beautiful woman, who used to pass our house carrying baskets full of washing."

"I don't know how you can remember such old things in such detail. . . . I can remember hardly anything of my childhood."

"That's because you live like a vegetable."

She did not lose her temper, but burst out laughing.

"All right, so now I'm a vegetable. . . . But what about Charles's father?"

"He was Swedish."

"What?"

"I tell you, he was a Swedish student, a boy from a good family, with a blond beard. . . . He was working for a shipfitter, learning the trade. . . . I only ever knew his first name—

Carl. . . . I'm convinced that even Charles's mother never knew his surname. . . . One day, he left. . . . Charles was born several months later, and his father probably doesn't even know he exists."

"In other words, the children may have a grandfather in Sweden?"

She poked the fire, then took a wooden spoon and stirred the onions sizzling in a saucepan. The air around them grew heavier. Laurence looked with a certain awe at this man with bright little eyes who was her brother, and who called forth such disturbing truths from the past.

"I can't get over it!" she sighed, sitting down again. "Are you quite sure?"

"Positive. Charles knows, too. . . ."

"He's never spoken to me about it."

"Have I ever spoken to you about Mama? Did you know that Papa left us for a year because he was having an affair with an Englishwoman and was planning to get a divorce and marry her?"

"That's enough, Paul!"

"Suppose Charles's father had stayed in Rouen a few months, maybe just a few weeks, more. He'd have found out his mistress was pregnant. He'd have taken care of the child. . . ."

"And Charles would be in Sweden now."

She suddenly started crying, without knowing why. It was almost as if her pipe-smoking brother had cast a spell on her, surrounding her with a warm fog that seeped into her body and softened every fiber. But the onions had something to do with it, too.

"Did you hear something?"

"No . . ."

"I thought I heard footsteps on the stairs. . . . I go and have a look ten times a day. . . . I put some water on the landing again. . . . And to think that he's Swedish . . ."

58

Then, without transition:

"Have you told Céline? . . . Listen . . . I'd like it if you didn't tell anybody. . . . I'm sure it would upset Céline to learn that when Mama was young, she . . ."

Come on! She had to snap out of it. She stood up, her cheeks wet.

"Would you like a drop of vermouth?"

"I'd prefer liquor."

"Wait . . . I'll see if there's any left."

There was a little at the bottom of the bottle.

"It's still no reason for him to lock himself in like this. . . . What's he hoping for? . . . He'll have to show himself finally. And then how's he going to look, I ask you? . . . A man with grown-up children playing a prank like this . . ."

The bell suddenly rang, echoing violently down the hall, and she jumped.

"Who could that be? . . . The milkman never rings."

Paul stayed where he was, with his feet on the stove and his glass warming in the palm of his hand. Laurence wiped her eyes as she passed the mirror and pushed back her tumbling hair a little. Near the stairs, she smoothed her hair: it had become a ritual, like crossing yourself in front of a crucifix. As she walked, she muttered:

"It's almost unbelievable. . . ."

She opened the door. There, right in front of her on the doorstep, stood the broad, stern figure of her brother-in-law Henri. It was so unexpected that she jumped again. He probably thought she was afraid. She tried to smile and murmured:

"Henri . . ."

He entered and was about to head for the kitchen. Without bothering to close the front door, she ran ahead of him.

"Henri . . . come in here."

Because of Paul! They had not spoken to each other for

years, though nobody knew exactly what had happened between them.

"In here . . . Is Elise well?"

She pushed him into the living room, forgetting that the folding door separating it from the kitchen was open.

"Are you alone?"

As he said this, Henri noticed Paul, still sitting in the wicker armchair, his feet on the stove. He said nothing, merely remained standing, his bowler on his head.

"Sit down . . . What's new?"

Poor Laurence, who so much wanted to be on good terms with everybody!

"Give me your hat. Take your coat off . . . Otherwise you'll catch cold when you go out."

It embarrassed her that Henri could see the little glass in Paul's hand. As if he were going to scold her for entertaining others better than she did him. But he was not the kind of man who would accept a little glass, so what could she do?

"You know he's still up there! This morning I put out some bread and water for him. . . . We took him up some hot coffee, but he didn't touch it. . . . Do you know what Mauricette says? That he must have a little stove in there, because she smelled coffee through the door . . ."

Which of the two would she prefer to see leave? Of course, Paul was her brother. On the other hand, Henri was rich and Charles's boss.

"Did you come by car?"

"I took the streetcar," he replied.

She did not like it that he could see how untidy the room was: plates with the remains of yesterday's cake, dirty cups and glasses.

"Do you mind if I go and check that nothing's burning?"

It was in order to face Paul and apologize with a glance.

60

Paul understood. He got up slowly, in a dignified manner. Bending over the saucepan with the onions, Laurence whispered:

"Come back later."

He was taking his time. It was almost as if he were going on a journey. He smoothed his beard in front of the mirror, brushed the brim of his hat on his sleeve, finished his glass of calvados, and finally declared:

"I'm off. . . . Good-bye, Laurence."

He could have gone out through the kitchen door and the hall. Instead, he deliberately crossed the living room in order to pass close to Henri, who did not flinch.

"Remember what I told you about Charles . . ."

What had he told her? Why did he mention it now? Doubtless for the opportunity it gave him to turn and face Henri, looking at him with eyes that appeared not to see him or to be staring at the wall.

"Good-bye, Paul."

She returned to her brother-in-law and untied her apron.

"Don't take any notice of the mess. . . . Paul arrived, and I didn't have time to wash up."

"I've come to talk to your husband."

"But . . . You know he's still locked in. It doesn't matter what you say to him, he won't answer. . . ."

Henri was undeterred.

"He hasn't been to the office for nearly three days now, and there are things that need to be attended to. . . . I don't know where he put certain papers. . . ."

"Are you annoyed?"

"I've come to talk to him."

She seemed to say:

"Go up if you like. . . ."

But he relighted his cigar and said distinctly, in his gravelly voice:

"I assume you've got shopping to do?"

"Me?"

Laurence never understood things immediately. With Paul, it didn't matter. But with Henri . . . From the way he looked at her, she felt she had made a blunder. She grew flustered, and quickly said:

"I mean, if you'd like to stay for a while, it'll give me a chance to get a few things. . . . Just imagine, I don't dare leave the house when no one else is here."

He stood and waited, just as he had waited for his brother-in-law to leave.

She ran upstairs, grabbed a coat, neatened her clothes as best she could. She forgot her purse, and had to go back up to get it. Then she rushed into the kitchen and stoked the fire, which was on the verge of going out.

"I'll be right back!" she announced. "Do you want anything? Are you thirsty? I can't offer you a cigar, because . . ."

Because there weren't any in the house. She was talking for the sake of it. She forgot her key again. She was outside before she realized this, but it was too late; she did not dare disturb Henri. She had no idea what she was going to buy. She did not need anything. Her cheeks were red, and she could feel the blood rushing to her head.

What had Henri come for? If she had left a little earlier, she could have caught up with Paul and talked to him about it, but he was sure to have gone too far by now. She had no reason to go into town. She was usually content to do her shopping in the neighborhood, claiming that the cost of the streetcar and the wear and tear on her shoes canceled out whatever savings could be made by going to the big market.

As she was entering the greengrocer's, she suddenly caught

sight of her brother, coming out of the tobacconist's, and she set off almost at a run along the sidewalk.

"Are you there, Charles?"

Henri knew very well he was there. As he had reached the top landing, he had heard a furtive noise from the attic, like the scurrying of mice. But he had to say something to start the ball rolling.

"You recognize my voice, don't you? Can you hear me? I assume you don't care to open the door . . . ?"

He was still wearing his hat and coat. The only thing he had left downstairs was his umbrella. The landing was in shadow.

"I've come to have a serious talk with you. . . . First, I want to ask you a question. . . . Do you know a woman named Sylvie?"

No reply. Henri felt ill-at-ease standing on the narrow landing, and he decided to sit on the top step of the stairs— a position he would not have liked anyone to catch him in.

"Don't be afraid. We're alone in the house. . . . I asked you if you know a woman named Sylvie. . . . I take your silence as an indication that you do. . . ."

A long silence. Henri was having difficulty breathing. It was his heart, which had been giving him trouble for a long time now, though he had never told anyone about it, and he had no desire to go to the doctor, for fear of learning the truth. That was the real reason he always let his cigar go out; it gave him the illusion of smoking without really doing so.

"Good! I thought as much. . . ."

What had he thought? That Charles would not answer him?

"I'm going to be quite blunt with you. You know that's the way I am. . . . If you don't understand, it doesn't matter,

63

but I have good reason to believe you will understand. . . . I'm ready to make a deal with you. Do you get my meaning? . . . I repeat, I'm ready to make a deal with you. . . .

"So that nobody will suspect anything, it would be better not to come out today. . . . People would make a connection with my visit. . . . Tomorrow or the day after, but within forty-eight hours at the latest, you can come and see me as if nothing had happened. . . ."

Silent laughter was naturally inaudible. Yet Henri had the impression that Charles was laughing like that, half opening his mouth but emitting no sound, and looking at the wall as if he could see through it.

"That's all I have to say. . . . You can name your own conditions. . . . I hope they're reasonable."

In the attic, a glass fell and smashed. Henri Dionnet was superstitious, and his reflex was to wonder if it was clear glass.

"Won't you say something?"

"No."

It was so unexpected that it scared him. Earlier, he'd been prepared to hear Charles's voice, but not just then.

And not that softly uttered monosyllable!

"I repeat, you have forty-eight hours. . . . I'm sure you'll be sensible."

He was in a hurry to leave. He thought he sensed danger around him.

"Good-bye, Charles."

He was already on the fourth step.

"Forty-eight hours."

He went downstairs, passed beneath the light with the colored-glass shade in the hall, and opened the front door. A second later, it closed behind him. He did not catch the streetcar at the first stop, near the grade crossing, but much farther on. He needed to walk.

64

A quarter of an hour later, Laurence, her basket on her arm, rattled the mailbox, looked through the keyhole at the empty hall, rang the bell, waited, and rang again. It was only half past ten, so there was nothing for it but to go into town, after all, and get a key from one of her daughters.

She thought of Lulu first, and found her kneeling, in her tight black dress, trying patent-leather shoes on a little boy. Laurence was not wearing a hat. Another assistant, who did not know her, offered to serve her.

"Thanks . . . I'm here to see my daughter."

"What do you want?" Lulu asked.

"Have you got your key?"

"So that's it! You forgot your key again."

She had to go into the back room and get it from her bag. The manager watched the two of them.

As soon as Laurence had left, and the lady with the little boy had been served, he called:

"Mademoiselle Lucienne!"

She walked toward him, ready to show her claws.

"Who was that?"

"My mother. She forgot her key. . . ."

"Try to see that it doesn't happen too often . . . The customers mustn't be kept waiting."

She had expected to be angry, but, instead, she smiled. He was looking at her, and she knew very well that what he was looking at were her burgeoning breasts beneath her black dress.

"Yes, monsieur!"

Chapter 5

SHE WOULD HAVE GONE OUT EVEN IF THEY HAD LOCKED HER in and she'd had to jump out the window. Not because she had anything in particular to do, but because she needed to get out. Besides, if anyone took the trouble to count, how many evenings a week, or a month, did the girls spend at home? Even that little hypocrite Camille had found shorthand classes as an excuse.

Lulu had been so exasperated at being watched so closely by her sister that she had finally stuck her tongue out at her across the table. Anyone would have thought, looking at Camille's wide eyes, that some catastrophe had happened to Lulu, that she was no longer a girl like any other, no longer one of the Dupeux family, but had been transformed into some kind of extraordinary creature.

Poor Camille! What dramas there would be when it was her turn! She had even followed Lulu into the dark hall and grabbed her arm as she was opening the front door.

"Where are you going?"

"What business is it of yours?"

"I forbid you to go. . . . If you go there again, I'll tell. . . ."

Lulu had shaken herself free, shrugged her shoulders, and flung her arms around like a puppet. Then she was outside, running toward the grade crossing.

She felt a need to stroll along the quay with Georges. Nothing more. And not even holding hands. Just strolling along, looking at the boats, stopping, pointing out the sights, stooping to pick up a stone . . . She was talking to herself. It was a habit. She was rehearsing phrases she would use in a while, unimportant phrases bearing no relation to what had happened.

It was half past eight in the evening when she crossed Boïeldieu Bridge. She noticed at once that Georges had apparently been waiting a long time. He was standing, not behind the newsstand, but at the curb, and he looked wryly at her, as if to say:

"You took your time!"

The quays, boats, logs and lumber, piles of all sorts of merchandise were to their left, but Georges took her arm and drew her straight ahead.

"Where are we going?" she asked.

This took place in the middle of a crowd, with streetcars and automobiles all around, and a traffic policeman four yards away.

"To our friend's place," Georges said in a low voice, pressing Lulu's arm with his fingers.

"We can't. . . . You told me he's always at home in the evening . . ."

She could see he was embarrassed. He looked down at the ground in front of him as he spoke and let fall a little laugh she did not like.

"What difference does that make? . . . His girl friend Lucette will be there. . . . We'll turn the light off. . . ."

They had just stepped off the sidewalk to cross the street. Lulu stopped dead, as if a car had suddenly appeared from nowhere. Abruptly, too, she turned to her companion. With her disheveled hair and bright eyes, she looked like some angry little creature, a bird or a fast-moving animal, a squirrel or a weasel.

"Dirty pig!" she managed to hiss. Something was rising in her chest.

"Hey, hold on . . ."

Lulu was almost inarticulate with rage.

"Dirty pig! . . . Dirty pig! . . ."

"Are you quite through?"

He shook her and, seeing that she was serious, all he could think of doing was to slap her across the face.

Lulu's reaction was quick. Twice, her hand, the long-nailed fingers curved into a hook, swooped down, scratching his cheek.

"That's it!" she concluded, turning and moving quickly away, half running, half walking.

She saw the policeman. She saw a streetcar stop almost beside her. She did not turn around. Once across the bridge, she began crying, in little sobs, repeating from time to time:

"Dirty pig!"

She had no handkerchief. She was always forgetting her handkerchief. The houses flashed past in the darkness. She bumped into a fat man, who turned to look at her as she ran on.

At least she had her key! She took off her shoes before opening the door. Despite everything, she made one of the stairs creak, and that idiot Camille appeared at the glass door of the kitchen.

"Is that you?"

"I'm going to bed."

It was time. No sooner was she lying on the bed, flat on her stomach and fully clothed, than she burst into raucous sobs, so loud that the pillow did not muffle them. She knew that she could cry like this for a long time, with her body shaking, a salt taste in her mouth, and the feeling that she was sinking into a bottomless pit. She had not turned the light on. There was only the reflection on the ceiling of a railway arc-light, filtered through the flower-patterned net curtains. A strange tremor ran through the house, making the walls and floors vibrate: it was Camille's sewing machine. She had bought material to make herself a new suit. Mauricette was also downstairs. She had given up her evening in order to iron her blouses, claiming that her mother did not do it well enough.

"Lulu . . ."

She froze. Her tears stopped. She did not dare look right away.

"Lulu . . ."

She knew he was there, her father was there. Through her spread fingers, she saw him now, standing in the darkness, with only his face and hands palely visible.

"Come with me for a minute. . . ."

She would have liked to sink deeper into her bed, to cling to it, to plunge into it. She was afraid.

"Come . . ."

Nevertheless, she obeyed. She felt almost dizzy. Swallowing her sobs, she followed her father up the dark staircase.

"Come in . . ."

She hesitated for a moment, as if it were dangerous to pass through this door that had been locked for days.

The sensation that took her breath away was a strange one; she knew this man she could not see was her father and yet she did not feel it. She was as frightened as if a stranger in the street had suddenly pushed her into a blind alley.

She found herself standing in an unfamiliar place; this was no longer the attic as she had always known it. The cabinet had been moved over and left just enough room for them to squeeze in through the door. There was a candle with a dancing flame, which reminded her of early Mass at church, with old women mumbling prayers in the surrounding darkness.

The most disturbing thing was seeing her father with a

beard, which made him look like Christ. She recognized him without really recognizing him. It seemed to her that she had never looked at him properly, that she knew nothing about him. He sat down on a crate. Next to it, he had made up a camp bed, which still bore the imprint of his body. Lulu felt like running away.

"Sit down . . . What have they done to you?"

She realized for the first time that she had stopped crying, but her cheeks were burning and her eyes were still teary. Her nose must be red and her lips swollen, which always made people laugh when she cried.

"Nobody's done anything to me."

To gain time, she looked around. Partly due to the candle flame, the room looked like something out of the Middle Ages, reminding her of books she had read long ago that had etchings showing a monk's cell or an alchemist's workshop.

And, with the white collar of his shirt open on his thin neck, Charles also looked different: younger, romantic.

"Sit down, Lulu. You seem frightened."

She shook her head vigorously. She was no longer afraid, but she did not feel at ease. The weirdest thing of all was the feeling she had that she was looking at her father for the first time. It was stupid, but she was suddenly unable to remember him without his beard, although that was how she had always known him, and if he had not spoken, she would have found it difficult to imagine the sound of his voice.

Wasn't he scrutinizing her just as curiously? She had not sat down. She did not want to sit down. She stood there, stiffly. A hiccup jolted her, and she had to sniff.

"Are you unhappy?"

She shook her head.

"Is it because of me?"

She shook her head again. Without reason, the desire to cry rose once more to her throat.

"Is it your mother?"

No! What was the use of all these questions?

"Someone else? . . . Your lover? . . ."

Her mouth opened. She was about to burst into sobs again.

"No!" she uttered through her tears.

She no longer knew where she was. Why was he tormenting her? Why was he looking at her like that? And what . . .

She turned, noticing that the hum of the sewing machine had followed her. Then the machine stopped. A voice was heard, clearly enough to be recognized as Camille's, though it was impossible to understand what she was saying. Mauricette said something in reply. The machine started up again. . . .

So the life of the house was audible here in the attic, its sounds carried up the chimney flues, which ran along the wall.

"Won't you tell me why you're unhappy?"

What business was that of his? He had never cared about her. Did anybody in the house ever care about anybody else? They all pulled in different directions, caring about nothing but eating and then right away going out. Except for Camille, who had taken a sudden interest in her sister, but only because she was no longer a virgin!

"What are they saying downstairs?"

She shook her head. She could not speak. How should she know what they were saying?

The panic she had felt earlier, when she had scratched Georges's face, came back to her.

"Has he done something to you? Is that it?"

Was what it? Was he talking, like Camille, about . . .

"Men are disgusting!" she suddenly cried, unable to stop herself. Her tears streamed again, and her nostrils flared.

She meant all of them, perhaps even her father, who was looking at her in surprise.

"Disgusting . . . dirty pigs . . ."

Why was he looking at her like that, almost without emotion? He seemed surprised, nothing more. And indeed, he now said, in that excessively soft voice of his, which he never raised:

"Is that all?"

"No . . . he wanted . . . he wanted to do it as a foursome."

She could not bear it any longer. Her fingers, her arms, her whole body wanted to writhe in pain.

She threw herself against the whitewashed wall, with her head in her hands, and wept distractedly.

He did not move. He did not go to her to pat her on the shoulder and try to console her. He looked at her back, clothed in black, her narrow neck, her unruly hair.

Despite her distress, Lulu heard furtive footsteps on the stairs. She thought:

That despicable spy Camille!

At that moment, there came the soft noise of slippers moving on the landing, and a muffled voice asked:

"Are you there, Lulu?"

Lulu wanted to wipe her eyes, but she still had no handkerchief. Everything disgusted her! She was furious!

Her father took a handkerchief from his pocket. "Give me!" she said impatiently, snatching it out of his hands.

Then she looked at him defiantly and said:

"Is that all you wanted?"

He did not know what to reply. With his ash-blond hair, his reddish beard, and the white blur of his open-necked shirt, he looked like an insubstantial shadow.

As Lulu shook her head angrily, her glance fastened on a perfectly material detail, a small can on one of the crates: a can of lobster!

She turned abruptly to the door, afraid it might be locked, and opened it.

72

"What are you doing there?" she shouted at Camille, who was cowering meekly in the darkness of the landing.

She went downstairs.

"Lulu!" called her mother, who was in her room, undressing.

"What?"

"What did he say to you?"

"Nothing . . . And you," she said to Mauricette, "why are you looking at me like that? . . . Is this your room? . . . No! So clear out!"

She gave Mauricette a push. Ten minutes later, she was lying in her bed, talking to herself in a low voice and staring at the light on the ceiling.

"Yes, I'll leave. . . . They won't be able to stop me. . . . I'll leave like Marie. And too bad for them if . . ."

Exactly! She would go on the street if she had to! She hated them all, especially her uncles and aunts. She would leave. . . .

Too bad if . . .

She stuffed the sheet into her mouth so that Camille, the despicable spy, would not hear her crying.

The next day was Wednesday, and Wednesday was not quite the same as other days. Bobinec had a sister in the suburbs, on the other side of the river. Her name was Julia. Her husband was a traveling postal sorter who was almost never at home.

She had given birth to a son two months before, and since then she had been ill and showed no sign of recovering. The family took turns visiting her, to look after her and do the housework. Wednesday was Laurence's day. She had to leave home early in the morning and did not return until evening. The girls ate in town.

It was a gray day, a day of inertia, a day when everything moved in slow motion, when you lived because you had to, out of habit, almost unconsciously, without savoring or enjoying anything. Laurence bought grapes for Julia, who lay in her bed, pale and damp, and spoke in a faint voice. She did a little washing, her favorite chore, then at five caught the streetcar back to town.

A detail she was to remember later was that she had thought of dropping in at Dionnet's. For no reason. To see her sister? Not really . . . The only thing that had made her change her mind was that she met her neighbor Madame Josse and decided to walk with her. She bought something at Josse's shop.

Back home, she lighted the fire and put water on to boil.

Strangely enough, she felt ill-at-ease. But she put it down to the cold and damp; the house had been unheated all day long. The air was raw. She looked at the clock, then went up to her room to undress. And frowned. It was a few seconds before she realized what it was that had struck her. A smell . . . The smell of shaving soap, of eau de cologne, which she never used. The wardrobe door was open, though she was almost certain she had shut it.

The foam on the shaving brush had barely dried. She looked up at the ceiling. Not waiting to finish washing, she started upstairs. She was a little afraid, and nearly waited for one of the girls to come back before she went any farther. But she was comforted by the fact that the attic door was open.

"Charles!" she called.

Her voice found no echo. The most extraordinary thing was that the attic had been returned to its old appearance. The cabinet was in its proper place, and the crates and old furniture were stacked against the walls.

"Charles . . ." she repeated, going downstairs.

The house seemed terrifyingly empty. Laurence caught herself murmuring:

"What's got into him all of a sudden?"

She almost went and waited outside, the way she had sat for hours on the doorstep when she was little, afraid to be alone in the house.

It was Camille who came home first.

"Your father's gone!" announced Laurence.

Camille was as stunned as she was.

"Gone where?"

"I don't know. . . ."

Laurence could not help making a little gesture with her hand and saying in a more light-hearted tone, now that she was no longer alone:

"Vanished!"

At that hour, Henri Dionnet was returning by car from Le Havre. He was not driving. His warehouseman doubled as a chauffeur whenever he needed to go somewhere, and he had been given a mouse-gray uniform.

Place du Vieux-Marché was all lighted up, its shops bustling with life. Before getting out of the car, Henri relighted his cigar and heaved a sigh, the sigh of an important man obliged to move.

He was in the habit of glancing in the shop windows from the sidewalk before he went in. The three assistants and Mademoiselle Thérèse were serving customers, principally country grocers who came once a week or once a month to get their orders filled. A wagon was just returning. Dionnet climbed the little stone staircase leading to the office. But he stopped before reaching the top, surprised to see a figure silhouetted against the glass.

It was Charles. There he was, in his place, bent over a ledger as usual, a green eyeshade on his forehead.

Dionnet turned and went back down to the shop.

"Mademoiselle Thérèse . . . what time did Monsieur Charles get here?"

"I didn't see him this morning, but he came on duty this afternoon, as usual."

"Did he say anything?"

"No."

"Has he seen Madame?"

"Madame hasn't been down."

Dionnet had to relight his cigar again. He sighed, wondering whether he ought to take off his bowler and velvet-collared coat first. No, he looked more solid and impressive with them on. At the door of the office, he took a deep breath and turned the knob.

But when he entered, Charles did not even look up. Henri coughed, walked up and down, shifted some papers, but no matter what he did, his brother-in-law remained absorbed in his work.

"I'm glad to see you've arrived!" Henri observed finally, playing with his watch chain.

"I'm sorry I was away, but I haven't been well these last few days."

What was that supposed to mean? Charles looked the same as ever, with the same calm, resigned, rather mournful expression, under the curly ashen hair.

"Tell me, Charles . . ."

It was obvious he was deliberately not reacting, deliberately remaining absorbed in the ledger. It was very hot. The office was always overheated; because of the glass partitions, the stove had to be kept going at maximum level, or else cold air swept in.

"Don't you think you owe us some explanation?"

"I don't think so," replied Charles, without looking up.

It was Henri who was out of his depth. He rolled his eyes.

"Oh, so you don't think so?"

"I said I was sorry, didn't I? I really was very tired. But now that I'm back at work . . . The accounts will be up to date by tomorrow evening."

"What about Sylvie?"

He stared straight at him, and Charles looked up. He had a surprised expression, the kind of expression that sometimes made people want to slap his face.

"Who's Sylvie?"

"Do you really not understand what I'm talking about?"

He was lying! But how could he get him to admit he was lying, when he was pretending to be so humble, so much the model employee? Even more than a model employee! He was overdoing it. Yet it was impossible to detect the smallest trace of irony on his face.

"No, I don't understand."

"And don't you think we have some things to settle? . . . Don't you remember certain letters written in colored ink?"

"Letters from whom?"

"In your desk at home there's a box of colored inks."

"Yes . . . I used them when the girls were still at school, to draw their maps for geography."

Henri had been prepared for anything but such an attitude, and, nonplused, he looked at his brother-in-law with a sort of awed respect. He felt almost as if he were seeing him for the first time, even though Charles had been sitting in the same spot, from morning to night, every day for more than ten years.

Laurence often said of her husband:

"He's as timid as a rabbit."

Elise, on her good days, when she was not drinking, would tell her husband:

"You shouldn't upset the poor man. He tries his best. . . . He's never had much luck in his life."

77

As for Martine, their daughter, who only set foot in the office to get money, she was fond of saying:

"Uncle Charles reminds me of a snail."

And what was it Paul had said about his brother-in-law—Paul, who cared so much about the origins of things, about their ins and outs?

"All right!" growled Henri. "I won't insist on it today."

He was furious, all the more so because he was scared. He could not make up his mind to leave the office, and he kept trying to catch his opponent's eye beneath the green shade.

"I thought it would all be much clearer. . . . After all, I'm a businessman! . . . I like things to be out in the open, cut and dried."

"I've just found the Valade contract," interrupted Charles, taking a file from one of the cabinets. "You were right. It wasn't registered. So if we want to avoid tax penalties, in case it's contested, we'd better . . ."

"Listen to me, Charles . . ."

"I'm listening."

"Leave all these papers . . . Look me in the eyes . . . How much do you want?"

"What for?"

"All right! Go on like that if you like . . . But I'll tell you this: your family isn't exactly well off, and your daughters have to work. . . ."

"What else do you expect them to do?"

"I'm willing to help you. . . . Let's say you wanted to set up in business for yourself somewhere."

"Thank you."

"Yes?"

"I don't have what it takes to go into business. . . . You've told me often enough that I lack initiative."

He smiled for the first time, or, rather, he showed his

78

teeth, which were close together and overlapped a bit at the front.

"So what *do* you want? How much?"

"What for?"

Henri was becoming hoarse. He dropped his cigar and crushed it angrily with his foot.

"As you wish . . ."

He walked to the door, stopped, and turned.

"Is that your last word?"

"Are you annoyed?"

The door slammed. Instead of going through the shop and the courtyard, Henri headed with heavy tread for the second floor of his house. On the landing, he met Elise, who announced:

"Have you seen him? He's back."

He passed her without replying.

"What's the matter?"

"Nothing!"

And he went and locked himself in his room, where he could be heard walking up and down.

At six o'clock precisely, Charles removed his eyeshade, closed the ledger, locked the file cabinets, put on his brown overcoat and beige hat, and headed for the street.

At half past six, as Lulu was waiting impatiently, as she did every day, for the shoeshop to close, she thought she saw her father passing by in the street, though she was not sure.

When the shutters were lowered a few minutes later, she broke with her usual habit and took the streetcar. She rushed into the house. Mauricette had only just got home and had not taken her hat off yet.

"Where's Father?"

"He's gone," sighed Camille, as if announcing a misfortune.

"When did he go?"

"Nobody knows. The attic's empty. He's put everything back in its place. . . ."

"He'll be back."

"What makes you say that?"

"Oh, just because."

"If that happens," said Laurence, "I won't have enough pâté. . . . Camille, will you go and get half a pound?"

Camille went to Josse's. An extra place was laid at the table.

"Did you see him?" they asked Lulu.

Camille came back. She was still in the hall when they heard the sound of a key in the front door. Charles stopped in front of the coatrack. His steps were as light as ever, almost slippery. He always seemed to be wearing very thin-soled shoes.

Nobody moved as he turned the knob of the glass door. Lulu wondered if he still had his beard; from the shop she had not been able to tell.

"Good evening," he said.

He looked at the laid table, at the stove, and at his wife, who had turned her head away.

As he sat down, he said the words his children had been familiar with since childhood:

"Shall we eat?"

Camille was giving her mother a severe look, to try to stop her from bursting into tears, since it was clear to everyone she was about to do so, for no reason. Lulu had sat down opposite her father, in her usual place, and was fiddling with a piece of bread.

"Was it worth the bother?" Laurence could not help saying as she placed the soup tureen on the table.

"Was what worth the bother?" he asked.

Again Camille looked sternly at her mother.

"Nothing! . . . How should I know? . . . I spent the day

at Julia's. The doctor came. . . . When I saw him to the door, he told me she has less than a month left. . . ."

And Julia gave her the excuse she needed to burst into tears.

"I wonder what her husband will do. . . ."

"Mama," Mauricette scolded her, "at least eat."

None of them dared look at Charles, who was slowly eating his soup. He had always been the last to finish.

"Have you got your class?" Lulu asked Camille.

"Yes, but I'm not going."

"Why not?" said Charles in surprise. "If you're taking a course, then you must go."

He looked at the pâté and asked:

"Is this from Josse's?"

Nobody saw one of his hands slipping under the table, the fist clenched painfully, the nails digging into the palm.

To top it all, they heard knocking on the mailbox. Lulu ran to open the door.

It was Paul, who asked loudly in the hall:

"Is he still up there?"

Lulu had no time to reply. Uncle Paul reached the kitchen door and muttered:

"Oh, I see. . . . You're here. . . ."

He nearly turned and walked away. He seemed in a bad mood as he turned to his sister.

"I just dropped in for news."

"Sit down a moment," Charles cut in, with his mouth full. "Have you eaten? How about a calvados?"

Paul was compelled to sit down. He did not know where to look.

"Julia's done for," announced Laurence.

There was at least that to fall back on.

81

Chapter 6

DID HE REALLY EXPECT ANYTHING? IT WAS VAGUER THAN THAT and largely unconscious. Expect what? Life in the house had already returned to normal. One by one the girls had come clattering down the stairs, with their hair and dressing gowns in disarray, and had, as so often, stood drinking their coffee or chocolate at the stove, warming themselves, their eyes still full of sleep but watching the rain against the windowpanes, so much rain that the kitchen seemed to be underwater.

Camille had two or three times cast an observant look at her father. She had greeted him with deliberate affection, trying to make him feel at home. She was a good girl, there was no doubt about it. But she was also the one he loved least.

Wearing a black oilskin and rubber boots, she had been the first to venture out into the deluge, in order to start work at the corset-maker's by eight o'clock. At that time, Lulu was still washing. Mauricette, half asleep, shouted from the top of the stairs that her milk was getting burned. And Laurence waited impassively for this morning hubbub to end; soon, when the house was empty, she would be able to sit down alone, lean her elbows on the table, dunk her bread and butter in her coffee, and slowly eat while reading her newspaper.

Charles bided his time, waiting until the last moment. He

knew Lulu was ready. Perhaps she was irritated that he was still there. He finally put on his overcoat, pulled galoshes on over his shoes, and took his umbrella.

The rain was coming down thick and fast in the half-light, pattering on the paving stones and bouncing off to a height of more than four inches, like flowers of spun glass constantly forming and dying. The railway crossing guard was wearing an oilskin coat that trailed on the ground. Water streamed in rivulets from the streetcar platform.

Charles turned around two or three times. No, the brown front door of his house was still closed. He walked along the street. All the others who, like him, were going to work from their homes in the suburbs and who at first were at quite a distance from one another in the streets, gradually, as they approached the bridge, formed a kind of procession. The surface of the Seine was barely visible through the misty rain. Bicycles passed by, the black backs of their riders bent over the nickel-plated handlebars; they rang their thin-sounding bells as they rode close to streetcars and trucks. Lulu walked past in the crowd, without seeing her father.

On mornings like this, the vast Dionnet establishment looked more than ever like a cargo ship glimpsed through the watery air, which was like the air of the open sea. At half past seven, old Poupin, the porter and night watchman, who also looked after the horses, would open the big gate, the draymen would enter and start harnessing the horses, and the warehousemen would begin rolling barrels and crates along the concrete platforms.

The warehouses were as huge as the holds of a ship and crammed to the ceilings. Signs read: NO SMOKING and TREAT THE ANIMALS WELL. One long vaulted room contained only barrels of herring; another, its roof pierced by trap doors, held nothing but coffee. And everywhere, pulleys and chains, and men in light blue overalls, with sacks tied around them like aprons, pencils over their ears, and order books stuffed with carbon paper in their hands.

At eight o'clock, little Mademoiselle Thérèse, whose small head was covered with bushy hair, would arrive, open the door of the wholesale shop to the assistants, and switch on the lights.

At half past eight, finally, it was Charles's turn. He would enter his glass cage, which was like a command post. Cold and damp would invariably greet him. Before taking off his overcoat, he would have to bend over the gas stove. The flame would come on, each time, with an explosion. A gas stove had been installed because the office was too small and got hot too quickly. The stove would be turned off for half an hour, then turned on again for ten minutes. The safe would soon be covered with damp steam. Charles would take off his jacket, put on an old one with threadbare sleeves, and place the green eyeshade on his forehead.

That was what should have happened—followed by the arrival of the two typists, who worked in an adjoining office, and then the appearance of Henri's squat figure, bowler pushed back on his head and unlighted cigar between his teeth, going from one wagon to another. He would say nothing, but observe everything with his hard eyes. The rain would be blackening the tarpaulins, which read: HENRI DIONNET—COLONIAL PRODUCE.

This morning, things did not happen like that. Charles closed his umbrella on the doorstep and entered the shop. Immediately, Mademoiselle Thérèse came toward him, her eyes wide and frightened.

"They're asking for you upstairs, Monsieur Charles."

Why was the scent of catastrophe in the air? Even the assistants' pasty morning complexions were more marked than usual, and they looked worried, like workers threatened with the possibility of being thrown out on the street.

"What's happened?"

As they crossed the shop, past its long counters and copper scales, the only words she could get out were:

"Monsieur Henri . . ."

He actually thought his brother-in-law was dead. The atmosphere was tragic enough for that, and the rain and lack of daylight, which still had not broken through, merely accentuated it.

He could not remember later what he had done with his umbrella, but he did remember, as he climbed the stairs, that there had been a car parked outside the door: Dr. Duprat's car, as he was soon to realize.

The housework had not been done. The door to the kitchen was open. There was a smell of medicine in the air.

It was Martine, Dionnet's daughter, who heard his footsteps, appeared in a doorway, and said wearily:

"This way, Uncle Charles."

She was as short as her father and looked rather common. She had not yet washed her face or done her hair. He entered the living room. The furniture was pushed into a corner, and the curtains had been taken down.

"Just when I'd started the spring cleaning," sighed Elise.

A cold wind blew in through the French windows, which were wide open on the stone balcony. Why had they opened the windows? It was as if they were all ill and needed fresh air.

"Come in, Charles . . . The doctor's in there. . . . He was here last night too. . . ."

She indicated a closed door. Dr. Duprat was behind it, with the patient. Charles was struck by how disordered the place was; it looked even worse than his own house. Nobody seemed to feel at home, nobody knew what they were supposed to say. The cook came in with some coffee and handed it to Martine, who tasted it and complained:

"There's no sugar in it!"

A maid emerged from the bedroom. As if her mind were on something else, Elise asked her:

"What does he say?"

"He wants some boiling water."

On a pedestal table was a dish containing a syringe and a used ampule.

"Well, isn't there any boiling water in the kitchen? . . . Oh, Charles, if you only knew what a night we've had! . . . It happened so suddenly. . . ."

She had not been drinking. That was clear from the fact that she had started the spring cleaning, always a good sign. But it only made her seem more distracted. It was obvious that she was slightly off-balance, and to steady herself she would soon enough go off and have a drink in secret.

Albert was there, too, which was rare. He was the only one who was fully dressed, in a gray suit and a light-blue tie. In normal circumstances, they almost never saw him. He was tall, at least a head taller than his father, and did not resemble him in the least. He was thin and had gentle eyes and measured gestures, as little like a Dionnet as it was possible to be. He was attending law school, because Henri was determined to make a lawyer or a judge out of him, preferably a lawyer, but he also belonged to a group of young poets, and he was ashamed of his family's wealth.

"I'll fill Uncle Charles in on what happened," he said. "Maybe he'll be able to tell us something. . . . Take your coat off, Uncle Charles."

Albert was the only one of the Dionnets who occasionally visited Laurence or Céline, as if he wanted to make up for his father's hardness.

"How's your mother?" Laurence would ask him, as he sat down at the stove as naturally as Paul and asked permission to smoke a cigarette.

"You know how she is," he would reply, without blushing. "Her life isn't very exciting, so she . . ."

The family was grateful to him for always finding an excuse for Elise.

He was not like Martine, who never visited any of her aunts and barely said hello if she passed one in the street. Of course, she spent most of her time with society girls or with English girls who came to spend a month with her and with whom she would then go to spend a month.

"I'd just been to the theater with Mother . . ." Albert was saying. He seemed more bothered than sad.

That was another thing they talked about in the family. Martine would never have taken her mother to the theater, not for anything in the world. Worse, whenever she entertained her friends, she was so afraid of a scandal that she locked Elise in her room. It was said that once she had even beaten her, because she was moaning in her room and could be heard in the living room.

"What's that?" one of the guests had asked.

"Nothing . . . A maid who's ill . . ."

So, Albert and his mother had gone to the theater. Martine had gone out too, with God knows whom—rich people, for sure!

"As we were leaving," continued Albert, "Father came down and went into his office."

In other words, into the glass cage, where Henri, who almost never sat down, had his own office, opposite Charles's, an office filled with green imitation leather.

"Mother asked him if he was going to do some more work."

Elise cut in:

"He didn't answer. I remarked to Albert that he was looking very strange. . . . I'd been noticing it for several days, ever since he went to your house the first time."

87

They fell silent, listening intently. There were voices in the other room, though it was impossible to make out the words.

"We could close the window!" said Martine, without moving.

Her brother went and closed it.

"We got back home just before midnight. He was still downstairs. He must have smoked a lot, because the office was blue with smoke. Mother asked him if he was coming to bed, and he said he would be right up. . . . But he was still downstairs when Martine got home a little while later. . . ."

Martine gave her uncle a harsh look and swallowed what was left of her coffee.

"Perhaps Uncle Charles knows what's worrying him," she said, frowning just like her father.

"Leave your uncle alone. . . . I was asleep when he came up, but was vaguely aware of him undressing and getting into bed. He pushed me, as he always does. . . . I noticed how cold he was. Then I heard him sighing. . . . I even asked him if the *tête de veau* was giving him indigestion. . . . He kept tossing and turning. It was keeping me awake. . . . Finally, I saw him standing in the dark, in his nightshirt. He was quite still. . . . I switched the light on.

" 'Turn it off!' he ordered.

"I switched it off. . . . I was starting to get frightened. I'd seen that he was clutching his chest with his hand, and his face was livid. . . .

" 'Are you ill, Henri? Shall I call the doctor? . . . What if I made you some herb tea?'

" 'Be quiet!' he said.

"He was still sighing. . . . I'd got used to the dark and I could see his eyes. . . ."

"That's enough, Mother. We've all understood," interrupted Martine. "He asked you to wake me, didn't he? Then he asked me to phone Duprat . . .'."

"He's a heart specialist," remarked Charles.

"He'd consulted him once before, last year, without telling us, while we were at the seaside. . . . Duprat admitted it last night. . . . We had to force Henri to go back to bed. . . . The doctor gave him an injection and came back this morning."

They automatically looked at the door.

"Martine claims her father is worried about something and that you must know what it is."

"I'm not the only one who thinks so; so does the doctor. He thinks Father has had a shock."

"It can only be something to do with the business," said Elise, somewhat indifferently.

"Do you know anything, Uncle Charles?" asked Albert gently.

Charles reddened. At that moment, he was seized with a sort of panic. Never had he felt so much a stranger as he did in this house. The sticky morning cold that had come in through the window had banished all intimacy. He would rather have been downstairs, in the haven of his glass cage, listening to the barrels rolling and the horses pawing the ground in the courtyard.

Suddenly the door opened, and Dr. Duprat appeared, with his bag in his hand. He was tall and thin, like Albert. He looked around, wondering who among all these people he should speak to.

Who, indeed, cared most about Henri Dionnet? Charles could have replied "Nobody!" Not even Martine; to her, he was simply the head of the family, and she found him a trifle unsophisticated.

"The worst of the attack is over," said the doctor, taking

89

his coat from a chair. "It may be a long time before he has another one. For the moment, he mustn't move, he must get plenty of rest, and he mustn't have any worries at all. . . . I've written a prescription. . . . Give him ten drops every hour in a little water with sugar. A little light vegetable soup about mid-day . . . I'll be back this evening."

"I think he's calling," said Albert.

Who would go? They looked at one another. It was Elise who made her mind up to answer. She left the door ajar, and they clearly heard his voice asking:

"Is Charles there?"

"Charles!" she called.

His legs almost failed him. He hesitated, his mouth dry, a worried look on his face. He walked to the door and heard Henri say to his wife:

"Leave us alone."

From one moment to the next, he found himself alone in the room with his brother-in-law, who ordered:

"Shut the door."

His voice was barely recognizable. He was having diffi-culty speaking. What struck Charles most were the two thick lines under his eyes, which gave him the appearance of having grown much thinner overnight. He pushed back the cover, revealing his beard.

Charles had never imagined his brother-in-law in bed. He was the kind of man you always thought of fully dressed, with his bowler and his cigar and the weight of his massive body, and with his clear-eyed look.

"Come here."

To save his breath, he gestured with his hand, a hand covered with brown hairs, drawing Charles to him.

"Are they all next door?"

Didn't his question reveal how frightened he was, deep down, frightened that, once he was bedridden, they would all desert him? And wasn't that what Charles had felt on entering the room?

Yes, they were all next door! But all the same, Henri was alone. Albert would go to his law lecture, just as Camille, on that memorable evening, had gone to her shorthand class. It was almost certain that Elise would continue with her spring cleaning. Once it was started . . . As for Martine, if she had an appointment with a friend . . .

It was as if Henri was gathering his strength before broaching the subject that mattered most to him now. He looked at Charles as if wondering what he could get out of such a man. Perhaps he dimly felt that he was a pitiful sight.

What were they whispering downstairs, those who feared for their jobs and wondered what would happen to the business if the boss passed away? They could already see the lowered shutters and the notices with black borders: "Closed due to death . . ."

And Dionnet, alone in his bed, was trying to take a deep breath and raise himself on the pillow.

"Come closer . . . In two days it'll all be over. . . . Duprat said so. . . . We must . . ."

He grimaced. The slightest effort gave him chest spasms. He lay motionless, listening to his heart beating.

"Do you know where she is?"

The moment had come. Was Charles going to keep denying it, pretending he did not understand? Would he dare persist in his stubbornness when faced with a defeated man?

"Listen . . . You can take what you like. . . . The key to the safe is in my waistcoat. . . ."

With a weak hand, he pointed to his waistcoat, on a chair where the previous night's clothes were piled.

"Take it . . ."

When Charles did not move, he repeated angrily, almost with tears in his voice:

"Take it!"

Charles, who had resisted so well the previous day in the office, and at the other times, in his attic, finally had no strength left. He took out the key, though it was of no use to him. Wasn't he richer than his brother-in-law? He had five hundred thousand francs! Nobody knew, but he had it! Of course, Dionnet's fortune was much larger, but Henri with his millions was not as rich as Charles with his five hundred thousand francs.

With all his millions, could Henri change his life? Hardly at all. Whereas Charles . . . He could buy a house in the country and retire. He could start a business. He could give his daughters better clothes than Martine's and send them to England just like her, instead of letting them sell shoes, dressed in black, or make corsets. . . .

"The combination of the safe is 'Marie.' "

He closed his eyes and put his head back on the pillow, so that his beard pointed up at the ceiling. The door opened noiselessly. It was Martine. She whispered:

"Can I . . . ?"

"Get out!" he cried, in a sudden burst of energy. "I want us to be left alone!"

And to his brother-in-law:

"Lock the door . . . Don't go away . . ."

He was trying hard not to dissipate what little energy he had left. He took his time, speaking slowly, in a hollow voice, as if dictating orders:

"Take what you need for yourself. . . ."

"I don't need anything," protested Charles, afraid of the sound of his own voice.

"Take as much as you like. . . . But you must take her some money. . . . Do you understand? . . . What have you done with the letters? . . . What does she say?"

And Charles, despite himself, replied:

"She's in Paris."

"How many times has she written? . . . How much does she want?"

His face suddenly contorted with pain. He was perhaps even sicker in mind than in body.

"It's for her daughter," said Charles, who was still holding the key to the safe, with no idea what to do with it.

"Take out whatever she's asked for . . . Take it to her . . . Tell her I'm ill . . . that I almost died . . . Tell her to wait until I recover."

He wasn't beaten yet—oh, no! It was clear that he would fight to the end, with all the energy at his command. But what Charles felt more than anything was that his brother-in-law was fighting alone, and that he knew it and was suffering from the void that surrounded him in his vast house.

"Will you go? . . . Listen, take the car. I'm so afraid she'll come here! . . . Tell Oscar to drive you . . . When you get back, come straight up here . . . What time is it?"

"Half past nine."

"Is everything all right?" asked Elise through the door.

Henri exclaimed impatiently. Was that how they saw fit to look after him? They were worried, they were confused, but for themselves, not for him. They could find nothing better to do than come and knock at the door. In another room, Martine, who was tired of waiting, could be heard taking a bath.

"Go!"

It was only then that Charles realized how familiarly his brother-in-law had been speaking to him today, as if he suddenly considered him one of the family!

"Will you come straight back? . . . Make sure you tell her . . ."

He was tired. He said again:

"Above all, see that the others leave me alone."

"You have to take your drops," objected Charles.

93

And Henri sneered back:

"Drops!"

"What did he say?"

"Nothing. It was about business."

"Always business!" sighed Elise. She had tied a kerchief around her hair to supervise the spring cleaning, and she was pushing the maids.

As Charles went out into the hall, the bathroom door half opened. He could see Martine's face, her shoulder, and the top of one breast.

"What did he say?"

He repeated:

"Nothing. It was about business."

Then Mademoiselle Thérèse, downstairs:

"Will he pull through?"

Even the draymen and warehousemen sent him questioning looks from a distance, wanting to know if Dionnet was still their boss.

Had Charles done the right or the wrong thing? At all events, he could not have acted any other way. It was not out of pity. He had observed his stricken brother-in-law coldly. Certainly, he had been a little disturbed to realize suddenly that Henri was alone, but that was a thought that had nothing to do with sentiment.

He weighed the situation, that was all. He saw a vast building for which three adjoining houses had had to be demolished, he saw wagons, workers, servants, a wife, a son, a daughter, stocks of merchandise, huge rooms full of sacks, and, in the middle of it all, Henri, struggling for breath, looking at him, him alone, and beseeching him:

"Will you go?"

It did not give him any pleasure to open the safe, which

was always full of money. He had as much money as he wanted, and he had no idea what to do with it. What could he do with five hundred thousand francs? He had thought about that for days and nights, in the attic.

In the end, he had done nothing at all. He had resumed his everyday life. Lulu was probably crouching in front of some peasant woman, trying on shoes. Camille was sewing in that gloomy room, dreaming of her shorthand teacher and worrying about her younger sister's exploits. As for Mauricette, as long as she could eat in expensive restaurants with her count . . .

Charles knew. He knew everything. He even knew that she had a fur coat at the office, which her boss had given her for their evenings together, but which she had not dared bring home.

And Laurence would soon be dropping in on Céline, or Paul, or . . . No, it was her day for her mother. The two of them must also be starting to tackle something like a spring cleaning.

"Is that you, Oscar? . . . Monsieur wants you to drive me to Paris in the car. . . ."

"Very good, Monsieur Charles . . . I'll just get changed. . . ."

Which meant exchanging his warehouseman's overalls for his gray chauffeur's uniform. Charles had no need to change his clothes. How much had Sylvie asked for in her last letter but one? Fifty thousand! She had the same kind of handwriting as young girls of good family who went to good schools, handwriting that for some reason sloped to the left.

My daughter is growing up. . . . I wondered what would become of her if anything happened to me. . . .

. . . I could . . . use the money to take out a life insurance policy, and then I could be sure that my daughter would never . . .

He took fifty thousand francs and no more. His own

money—Laurence would have been astonished—was hidden in the attic, on top of the cabinet, all in thousand-franc notes, held together with elastic bands.

Laurence slept beneath a real fortune! So did the girls! Even Lulu, who had her movie tickets paid for by some nobody named Georges and who would run after her sisters to borrow money from them for the streetcar.

It was easy to understand why Charles had married Laurence. He had no family and had been brought up in an orphanage. He had always been alone. And Laurence, even at the age of twenty, had mothered him. Whenever he became sentimental, she would burst out laughing.

"You *are* funny, Charles! If you only knew how funny you can be, when you make a face like that!"

But Henri? He had always known, even when he had arrived in Rouen and had lived in a room without gas or electricity, that he would amount to *something*. He could hardly not have noticed how happy-go-lucky the Babin family was. Paul at that time had been the same as he was now. Céline at sixteen had been like Lulu, just as uncontrolled, except that, instead of going to the movies, she would go to an open-air dance hall, jumping out the window with her shoes in her hand if her mother had forbidden her to go out. Today she had five children!

Elise was beautiful, that was a fact. She was the best-looking of the Babin girls. . . . She had not started drinking yet. It was said in the family that she had started only when, after her first baby, she had been prescribed stout as a pick-me-up.

And since then Henri had worked as hard as he could to establish himself.

"The car's ready, Monsieur Charles. . . . I'll just have to stop on the way for gasoline. . . . If it keeps on raining like this, we won't go fast. . . ."

He wondered whether to sit beside Oscar. But Oscar had already opened the rear door for him. He had forgotten his umbrella, but never mind.

"Do you want to let your family know? I can drop you at your house."

He was being treated with kid gloves. He was the boss's brother-in-law, but he was also an employee and he lived in a little house in the suburbs.

The feeling of emptiness he had had in the house on Place du Vieux-Marché pursued him through the streets and onto the main road. It was the weather! These were hours not worth living through, hours you endured while waiting for something better, like hours spent in a station waiting room, staring gloomily at trains passing and umbrellas dripping.

What depressed him most was what he saw along the road: a brick gable with a huge painted advertisement, dark rivulets of water, chickens behind a wire fence pecking at the black earth or the soaking dunghill, rabbits sitting resigned in their cage.

Cars went by in the opposite direction—people behind the windshield wipers, sprays of water thrown up by the wheels—then they passed a string of boats, a tug sounding its siren furiously on the vast gray expanse of the Seine, a metal bridge, and a man fishing from a punt anchored in midstream.

Oscar opened the window between them and half turned.

"Which part of Paris do you want? . . . It's so I know which road to take, to avoid traffic. . . ."

"Rue Notre-Dame-de-Lorette," he said.

A train whistle blew. Rails stretched a hundred yards across, in a sort of wasteland dotted with apparently abandoned railway cars. On the shoulder of the road, an old man was walking, bent double, a sack on his back.

He had to make an effort to imagine that in a second- or third-floor apartment in a house on Rue Notre-Dame-de-

Lorette, Sylvie was opening the door to her clients, smiling at them, calling them "my little pet" or "my wicked boy," ushering them into a room where a cat lay purring on a couch, and clapping her hands and calling:

"Come in, ladies . . ."

This, while taxis cruised and buses with opaque windows went by on the sloping street.

Chapter 7

A VIOLENT GUST OF WIND BLEW THROUGH THE ENTRYWAY. AT the far end of the courtyard were a hairdresser's and a chair-mender's. On the brown walls, enamel nameplates indicated the tenants' professions and black hands or arrows pointed to Staircase A or Staircase B.

Madame Sylvie, masseuse, was on the third floor, to the left, and when Charles stepped on the doormat, a bell rang in the apartment before he had even pressed the button. There was a sound of laughter.

"Quiet, ladies!"

The door opened, merely a crack at first. The visitor was looked up and down; then the door opened wider and a round pink face appeared, lighted up by a smile.

"Come in . . . This way . . ."

Although she did not stop smiling, she was obviously racking her brain to try to remember him; finally, she had to ask:

"Have you been here before?"

"I'd like to speak to Madame Sylvie. . . ."

"I'm Madame Sylvie."

She frowned and glanced at the door.

"Henri Dionnet sent me. . . ."

"Oh . . ."

This time she was really suspicious, which was rather comical; seriousness did not suit her aging doll's face, with its lack of wrinkles, its enamel complexion, and her tow-colored hair.

"Has something happened to him?" she asked.

Then she changed her mind and stood up.

"Will you excuse me a moment?"

The room she entered, closing the door behind her, was pregnant with silence and suspense. No doubt that was where the women waited, and Madame Sylvie was going to inform them that he was not a client. But a bell called her away, to one of the bedrooms. Then she saw a man out, as far as the landing, having regained her smile, and when she opened the reception-room door again, Charles caught sight of a naked woman passing in the dark hall, one hand on her stomach.

He waited without moving, sitting on a gilded chair near the stove, its flames visible through mica windows. There was a little nickel-plated basin containing hot water with rose petals floating on it, and carefully draped, cream-colored satin curtains, which completely hid the outside world. It was very warm, a special, almost furry warmth. Seven or eight cushions lay scattered on the divan, and the walls were decorated with erotic prints. The light, soft and intimate, came through a shade in the shape of a doll's crinoline.

"Please forgive me . . ."

It was unlikely that Sylvie's apartment in Rouen had been as comfortable as this. But had it had this velvety atmosphere, full of the whispering and rustling of figures hidden behind doors and walls? If so, the strange thing was picturing Dionnet, so massive and hard, with his beard and his bowler and his clothes that looked as if they were cut out of solid matter, standing on the doormat that rang, walking down the unlighted hall, and finally sitting on one of these fragile chairs.

Sylvie asked no questions. She waited discreetly, scrutinizing him from time to time. Nevertheless, as Charles crossed and uncrossed his legs but still said nothing, she was compelled to break the silence and murmur:

"Is he well?"

"He's very ill. . . ."

"Is that why he hasn't answered my letters?"

"I'm his brother-in-law," he declared, as if that were significant.

"Oh!"

That was obviously not what she had been expecting. She watched his hands as he took his wallet from his pocket.

"I've brought you money."

After the bare road, the rain, the wind, the bustle of the streets, he was suddenly soaked in warmth and peace. Sylvie had sat down again in front of him and crossed her plump hands in her lap. He noticed that she was wearing expensive high-heeled shoes and that her feet were very small, with high insteps.

"Fifty thousand, wasn't it?" he murmured, handing her five wads of notes.

She quickly grabbed them, looked around, and, doubtless deciding that there would be time later to put the money in a safe place, simply slipped it into the drawer of a dressing-table.

"Will you have something to drink?"

My goodness, yes. He had no desire to leave. He felt good here, like someone relaxing after a long run.

"Some champagne? . . . Yes, I insist! Especially because you came all the way from Rouen."

Once again, she half opened the door, and once again Charles felt the warm breath of the human life crammed into the other room.

"Bring us a bottle of champagne."

She came back. She was happy, but a little embarrassed.

"I was surprised that a good friend like him didn't reply. . . ."

She would have liked to make sure how much he knew.

"Is it really serious? . . . Will he recover? . . . "

"This time, yes, but the next attack . . ."

"His heart, isn't it? . . . I've noticed it's often very strong men who die of heart disease. . . . Come in, Sophie. Put the tray down here."

A nondescript maid, dressed in black, with a white apron, leaned over and said something to her employer in a low voice.

"Tell him I'll be right there. . . . Will you excuse me?"

Another client, in one of the rooms. It took a long time. Presumably something had not gone right. And the client was obviously dissatisfied with the explanation, because the door of the apartment was slammed shut.

Nevertheless, Sylvie was still smiling when she returned.

"What was I saying? . . . Oh, yes, I was talking about the heart . . ."

She uncorked the bottle and filled the glasses.

"Your health! I was planning to go to Rouen and see him one of these days. . . ."

"I know."

She gave a start, looked at him more closely, and waited. He said quietly, with malicious pleasure:

"I've read the letters."

She almost guessed, from his attitude, that he had them in his pocket, which was true.

It had happened in the most innocent way possible, on a day when the stock market was open in Le Havre. On such days, Henri left first thing in the morning, and it was Charles who opened the mail. In theory, he did not open private letters, only those with names or return addresses he recognized. He had slit open an envelope with the paper knife and had read:

102

Monsieur,

It's been a long time since I last got in touch with you, though I know how well disposed you are toward me. Since I wrote to you last year from Nice, I've moved to Paris and started work again.

It would have been nice to have a visit from you, but I know how busy you are. I'm therefore obliged to inform you of my plan by letter, and I'm sure you will give it due consideration.

So far you've always helped me when I've asked you to, and the small amounts I've needed have been quite enough for me.

My daughter is growing up. I've placed her in a boarding school in Belgium, and I visit her from time to time. The last time I was there, I wondered what would become of her if anything happened to me. That was when I thought of you.

Couldn't you give me one quite large lump sum that would rid me of all worries in this matter? I could go to a reliable insurance company and use the money to take out a life insurance policy, and then I could be sure that my daughter would never know what it is to be poor.

Can you send me fifty thousand francs for this purpose? For my part, I promise never to ask you for help again.

You can see how reasonable I'm being. You know I've always been reasonable, and you also know you can count on my discretion. . . .

Charles had slipped the letter in his pocket, for no particular reason other than that his brother-in-law would have been angry to discover he had opened it.

It was only gradually, at odd moments, sitting in his glass cage, that he thought about it. Every morning when the letters arrived, he would glance at them automatically, and one day he recognized the handwriting.

He had not hesitated.

Monsieur,

I am surprised not to have received any reply to my letter of last month. I do think my proposal was a reasonable one and that anyone else in my position would have taken greater advantage.

Remember those times you used to come and see me on Rue du Chaudron with your friend. . . .

I would like to think that you won't forget an old friend who is only claiming a very small part of what she helped you gain and . . .

It was not until the third letter that Sylvie became more explicit.

. . . I really can't understand your silence and I prefer not to think that you've forgotten the service I did you. I wonder what would happen if I were as big a gossip as some women. You're lucky I'm not more acquisitive.

But I'm not stupid either, and there are quite a few things I've understood. For instance, that if your friend hadn't died, you would surely not be the important businessman you are today.

Yet what have I got out of it, after all the trouble I went to? Ten thousand francs on one occasion, then three money orders, for five thousand each.

Now I'm asking you for fifty thousand, once and for all, and you're very deliberately not replying.

I'm wondering whether I will have to contact someone who can advise me. I'll only do that as a last resort, if you continue to ignore me.

*Otherwise you know you can always count on my silence
and that I remain your devoted*

Sylvie

She was smiling as she held her glass in her doll-like hand.
She appeared not to be thinking, and yet she was clearly keeping her ears open for the slightest noise in the apartment. It
was she who had written the final note, in the same backward-
sloping, respectable schoolgirl's handwriting.

*If I don't get a reply within a fortnight, the Bonduel family
(I've made inquiries and there are still brothers-in-law, who
were very surprised to have inherited only a pittance) may well
learn how Jean Bonduel died and how a gentleman of my
acquaintance brought him to my house almost every night in
order to slowly kill him.*

The extraordinary thing was that Charles had known all
along, just as he knew about Mauricette's schemes involving
the count, just as he knew about Camille's pitiful sentimen-
tality, just as he had guessed all about Lulu's dirty little affair.

He had known Jean Bonduel when he was Dionnet's partner. He had seen him in the office, light-hearted and frivolous,
lacking in substance, with pink cheeks and bright tubercular
eyes.

He knew the two men often went out together in the
evening.

And now, in Sylvie's reception room, he saw it all! That
was it. It was so simple. Almost too simple.

Perhaps in the beginning it had not been deliberate on
Henri's part.

Charles would have liked to see the men who were pressing the bell under the doormat and whom he could hear whispering in the bedrooms. Were they like his brother-in-law?

Yes, that was it! Henri must have been in the habit of visiting Sylvie when she was living in Rouen. Charles could imagine his broad back on the staircase as he left, buttoning up his heavy overcoat and searching in his pocket for a cigar.

Was he the one who had introduced Bonduel to Sylvie? And was he the one who had then had the idea? More likely she! It was the kind of idea that would occur to a woman like her, a woman used to seeing men before and after, being confided in by their partners, perhaps listening at doors.

For instance, she might have said to Dionnet:

"Your friend's a real stallion. . . ."

Or some such word used in places like this.

"At this rate, he'll soon burn himself out. . . ."

Weren't consumptives particularly passionate?

There! It was quite simple. They just had to give him a little push. . . .

"You're not drinking," she observed. "What are you thinking about?"

What had *she* been thinking about? Obviously about what formed the basis of her profession. She seemed a little hesitant.

"I wonder if I might suggest . . ." she said in a low voice.

She studied Charles. Why not? After all . . .

". . . Would you like some of my little ladies to join you for a drink? I have some very nice ones. . . . You will say yes, won't you? . . . So that you won't have come all the way from Rouen for nothing."

Without waiting for an answer, she opened that familiar door.

"Louisette . . . Geneviève . . . Marcelle . . ."

They came in. They were well behaved and almost shy. They shook hands with him, and Charles wondered if one of them was the woman he had seen stark naked in the hall. They were fully dressed. One of them was wearing a charming navy-blue suit.

106

"Take your glasses, girls. Monsieur is a good friend of mine. . . ."

Which obviously meant:

"You must be very nice to him. . . ."

Then, with a conspiratorial smile:

"Will you excuse me? I think someone's calling me."

To one of the women, in an undertone as she was leaving:

"The blue room . . ."

Charles did not protest. He was still thinking about Henri, wondering if he had kept up the habit of visiting someone like Madame Sylvie in Rouen. Very likely he had.

It was extraordinary how far away everything seemed. The rumbling of the buses could still be heard, yet it was hard to believe that the street was there behind the curtains, with its floods of water and its black-clad figures rushing past.

The apartment was really like a world apart, a world where the warmth was not the same as elsewhere, where the air had a different feel, the voices a different resonance, where strange words were uttered, or words that took on a different meaning, where it seemed quite natural to see a tall brunette undress and light a cigarette as she sat down on the arm of a chair.

"Are you from Rouen?"

She asked that because Madame Sylvie had introduced him as an old friend. And she had lived for a long time in Rouen. . . .

"I'm from right near there: Bréauté."

Like the Babin family. Like Laurence. They were really pleasant, all three of them, full of good humor and willingness to please. Didn't they spend all day dressing and undressing in this soft atmosphere?

Perhaps Marie . . .

"What are you thinking about?"

"Nothing . . ."

He was thinking about Marie. And now he could think about her calmly, almost coldly, unlike Laurence, who, whenever her eldest daughter's name was mentioned, felt she had to sigh and turn her head away as if she were about to shed a tear.

For Charles, that was long past. And yet he had been a normal father. Many was the night, when Marie was very little, that he got out of bed to make sure she was tucked in properly. He heated her bottles and sang nursery rhymes to put her to sleep. He proudly pushed her carriage through the streets, and he was the one who went with her the day she started school.

Perhaps he had not cared enough about the other children as they were growing up because he had had eyes only for Marie?

"Your pet," Mauricette would say, jealously.

He found it difficult now to call that period to mind, and especially to see himself as he was then. He could not have changed much in appearance. By and large, he was a man like the men you saw everywhere in the street, a husband, a father, an ordinary employee, who remembered everyone's birthday and name day and bought cakes, and who came home on Christmas Eve with his arms full of packages.

His brother-in-law, at that time . . .

It was the period of Sunday-afternoon card games. For some reason, life went in periods. There was the period when they all met at Bobinec's and the period of trips to the country. There had even been a period when the whole family had taken up fishing.

The card games were with Monsieur Chaigneau. He lived two doors away. He was thirty-five, unmarried, and worked for the tax department. People looked up to him because he had a housekeeper, which was unusual in the neighborhood.

For months, the whole family swore by him, even Paul, who tended to be suspicious.

"Monsieur Chaigneau said so. . . ."

"Go and ask Monsieur Chaigneau if he's coming tomorrow. . . ."

They went to him for the smallest thing. He would drop in to say hello and bring them magazines.

One evening, returning from the office, Charles had seen his door ajar and had pushed it open. Why was it that Charles never made any noise? He was not silent by intent, and certainly not in order to take people by surprise. He could still see the blue-tiled hall and the door; also ajar, of the living room, where there was a piano and an adjustable stool covered in red plush.

That was where he had seen Monsieur Chaigneau and Marie. Marie was not yet sixteen! And what they were doing, in the semidarkness of the room, was not something simple and normal. It was ugly. . . .

He had said nothing. He had left without a sound, and had never spoken about it to anyone. And it would perhaps be an exaggeration to claim that from that day he had changed.

"Why are you looking at Monsieur Chaigneau like that?"

Finally, Monsieur Chaigneau left, because he was transferred to a post in the suburbs of Paris. Marie lived at home for another two years. Then she got it into her head to go to Paris and work as an assistant in a department store.

"Aren't you going to stop her? Why don't you say anything?"

No! Why should he? He knew! And not only about the Chaigneau episode. There had been others, including a local policeman Charles still saw from time to time on duty on Boïeldieu Bridge.

"Aren't you going to undress?"

He wondered whether or not to undress. He had not made up his mind. Wasn't it strange to think that that was the way Jean Bonduel had died? A rich, carefree young man, who, as

Laurence said, had had everything anyone needed to be happy!

That someone like him should have fallen in with a man like Henri! . . . What had the Bonduel brothers-in-law to say about that, certain as they had been up until then of inheriting?

"You'll see, he'll be fleeced by that Dionnet. . . ."

Of course! How could that idle boy have hoped to keep up with his partner's dealings? He had seen the money coming in and the business booming. He had believed in it.

When he died, there had barely been enough left in his account to pay for the funeral.

Charles was sure that Madame Sylvie was listening at the door. He had sharp ears and had made out a rustling sound. Perhaps she was even looking through the keyhole? As she had with Henri . . .

One of the women was surprised.

"Don't you want to . . . ?"

No. All things considered, he wasn't in the mood. Besides, he had never been very keen on love-making.

"It's time I went. . . ."

"Just like that?"

Yes, just like that! Sylvie came in, which proved she had been listening at the door.

"So soon?"

"Yes. I must get back to Rouen."

"Leave us, girls . . ."

Then, in a more serious voice:

"Do you really think something might happen to him? I'm asking you that because . . ."

Come on! Because what? Because she had something at the back of her mind, obviously. Charles said nothing, but he guessed.

He had sometimes wondered if he was really a man like any other, or whether he had a sixth sense. He knew, for example, that a minute earlier one of the women had winked behind his back, although he had not seen her in a mirror and a wink made no sound. How could he know? And how could he have known what had happened to Lulu, when he had not followed her or even seen her? She could have been crying for some other reason. But no! He had been expecting it. He had been aware for days that it was bound to happen.

"You're his brother-in-law, did you say?"

Sylvie was wondering if, in his capacity as brother-in-law, he was defending Dionnet's interests, or if, on the contrary . . .

If Henri was going to die, wouldn't it be sensible to take advantage before it was too late?

That was what she was thinking. That was why she was hesitating and playing with her key.

"Won't you come back to Paris one of these days? . . . I hope the girls were nice to you? . . ."

"Very nice."

"Tell him I thank him and wish him a speedy recovery."

She sighed. It was a pity to miss a good chance, but she was suspicious of Charles.

"Are you going back by train?"

She saw him out, after making sure there was nobody in the hall or on the stairs.

"I've got the car downstairs. . . ."

"Good-bye . . . When you want to . . . Don't be shy."

He went down to the drafty entryway, the rain, the shiny car, and Oscar coming out of a bar, wiping his mustache.

"Back to Rouen?"

"Yes, back to Rouen."

He looked up, but all he could see on the third floor were closed blinds. It was over. The road . . . They almost knocked over a bicyclist, who swerved, and Charles lived through the accident in the smallest detail, as if it had really happened. He noticed that Oscar, who had been drinking, was driving in an exaggeratedly devil-may-care fashion, and from that point he could not take his mind off the dangers of the road.

The streetlights had long been on by the time they reached Rouen, but the shop was still open. Mademoiselle Thérèse was weighing kidney beans.

A strong smell of beeswax pervaded the staircase. It came from upstairs, where they were just finishing restoring the living room to normal.

"Is that you, Charles? . . . He's already asked for you three times. . . . If we'd let him, he'd have got out of bed."

The crisis was over. Henri had not died. So they regarded him as a normal man again. He had asked for the door to be left open, in order to hear what was going on. He was sitting in bed propped up by two or three pillows.

"Shut the door . . . Did you see her?"

"It's done," Charles merely said. "I gave her the fifty thousand francs."

"Did she say anything?"

A simple shake of the head. No, nothing. And now Henri did not know what to say either. Here they both were, looking at each other in silence.

And this was just the beginning. It was from this moment that things were going to get really bad.

"Laurence was here. . . ."

Because he had not come home for lunch, of course! It was of no importance.

"Have you been to the office?"

"Not yet."

There were other questions Henri would have liked to ask, but Charles knew quite well he would not dare. He looked coldly at his brother-in-law, at his colorless cheeks above his beard and his eyes with two dark lines under them. He knew he was being cruel, but what did it matter?

"Don't forget to go to the bank tomorrow morning for the Pénicaud bill."

Neither Martine nor Albert was at home.

"Good night!"

He crossed the living room, where his sister-in-law had been helping the maids put the furniture back in place.

"Are you going? Laurence was here. . . ."

"I know."

"Did he say anything? . . . The doctor'll be here any minute. . . . Don't you think he's better?"

"Definitely."

He went into the shop and repeated to Mademoiselle Thérèse:

"He's better."

He found his umbrella at the foot of the stairs and opened it as he stepped out onto the sidewalk. He walked along, past lighted shop windows, like hundreds of other employees on their way home, their day's work finished.

Chapter 8

IT WAS AUTOMATIC. HE HAD ONLY TO UNBUTTON HIS OVER-
coat in order to get his key from the right-hand pocket of his
jacket, and to move his head slightly forward, barely lowering
it, until his eyes were at the level of the keyhole. He did not
need to get close. The hall seemed very long, an endless neutral
space feebly lighted through the colored-glass shade. At the
end of this vista, the light at the kitchen door seemed fierce.

People who saw scenes from the past or the future in a
crystal ball probably saw them like this. The door, too, with
its sixteen rectangular panes of glass, was quite small, and
nearly always the figure of Laurence could be seen behind it,
in her usual place.

But it was a Laurence who seemed both terribly familiar
and terribly distant, in time as well as in space, a Laurence
who was knitting, or eating, or speaking, or, rather, moving
her lips noiselessly as she addressed unseen people in another
part of the kitchen. Nearly always, at the moment the key
clicked against the metal of the lock before being inserted, she
turned her face toward the no-man's-land of the hall, her lips
moved, and it was obvious she was saying:

"There's Charles."

That was not the only obvious thing. It was also obvious
that something had stopped, that life had changed, because

Charles had come home. The conversation was not resumed, or else they quickly changed the subject. Perhaps they even hid whatever had been on the table, so that he couldn't see it. And they probably sighed, there at the back of the house, because the warm, cocoonlike atmosphere in which they had been snuggling would now be broken.

It was almost the same at other times, with the girls moving around the house, running, singing, calling to each other from room to room, arguing with each other on the stairs, slamming doors. The sound of his key in the lock did not put a stop to all this excitement, but the activity did lose its joyful, uninhibited character.

"There's Charles."

He advanced softly to the coatrack, took off his overcoat and hat, and put his umbrella down so that the water could drip off it. This time, he sniffed, because the house was filled with the pungent smell of herring, which he had never been able to stand. Perhaps Laurence was tempted to remove them from the table, but she did not have time, and the kitchen was still blue from the grease in which the herring had been fried.

They were eating without him: Laurence's mother, whose day it was, Laurence, and the three girls. And Laurence, who could see he was not in a good mood, said in a cheerful voice, with that slight tremor of the lower lip she always had when she was not being sincere:

"You obviously didn't feel like having a good time in Paris! . . . From what I was told at Henri's, I thought you'd be back late."

She went to the cupboard to get the black pudding she had bought for him, in place of the herring. He merely said good evening and sat down at his place. The others seemed to have lost their appetites and the thread of their thoughts.

Laurence, nevertheless, resumed:

"What were you saying, Mama?"

This time, Charles was certain there was a sort of conspiracy against him. He noticed that Camille had the inflamed eyelids of someone who had been crying and a strange brightness in her look. He also caught the glance Laurence gave her mother, and he could see how embarrassed and clumsy the old woman had become in her son-in-law's presence.

What had he done to them? He was always so unobtrusive and he never stuck his nose in their business. With Paul, it was even worse. As soon as Charles appeared, Paul, sitting by the fire, would fall into an unpleasant silence; then, after rarely more than five minutes, he would sigh and announce:

"I must go. Good-bye, Laurence."

And to the others:

"Good-bye, everyone."

"What was I saying?" asked the old woman now. She had stopped eating.

"You were talking about Arthur. . . . About how he'd quit his job . . ."

She was annoyed at her daughter for forcing her to continue in front of Charles.

"He says he used to get his clothes dirty and wear out his shoes for only thirty francs a day. . . ."

"What's he going to do now?"

"If he can manage to borrow five thousand francs, he'll buy an old truck that's for sale in his neighborhood. . . . He's sure that by going and collecting vegetables from the outlying farms and bringing them in to market . . ."

Laurence's big eyes seemed to look deep into the past.

"Didn't Papa collect vegetables at one time?"

How could she ask that with Charles here? Her mother corrected her:

"That wasn't the same. . . ."

"Oh! . . . And where does Arthur plan to get the five thousand francs?"

116

Arthur spent his whole life looking for money, whether five thousand or fifty, to eat, to pay the doctor's bills, or to start a business.

"He talked to Bobinec about it and offered to make him a partner. . . . But right now even Bobinec . . ."

"Where are you going?" Laurence asked her husband.

He had stood up. Without answering her, he left the kitchen. Laurence frowned, wondering what had got into him this time, especially when she heard him climb all the way up to the attic.

Mauricette seized the opportunity to leave.

"Will you be home late?" asked her mother.

"I don't know."

"Don't you think that on a day like today . . ."

She looked at Camille. Mauricette shrugged.

"There's nothing I can say that . . ."

She was closing the front door when Charles got back to the kitchen, his face as blank as before, and placed five thousand-franc notes in front of his mother-in-law. Old Madame Babin laughed nervously.

"What are you doing?"

"It's for Arthur."

Laurence, with that boisterousness she always showed when she was confused, burst out:

"So you're rich now, are you, Charles?"

Lulu looked at her father. So did Camille.

"Well! Give Arthur the five thousand francs, Mama. . . . As long as Charles hasn't stolen it . . ."

The two women talked a little more, for the sake of talking, about Céline's second son, who had the mumps. Charles continued eating in silence, like a rabbit. He knew it was not over yet. He wondered anxiously what was coming next. It made him feel physically ill to think about it, as did everything that disturbed the humdrum calm of his life.

If it had been possible, he would have slipped noiselessly into the other room and buried himself in some work or other—in the same way as, after Marie had left, he had taken a clock apart, piece by piece, and then spent more than a year putting it back together again.

Laurence must have sensed that Charles was planning his getaway. She looked at Camille. Camille began to clear the table, without looking anyone in the face.

"By the way, Charles . . ."

That meant it was serious.

"Camille's afraid to tell you about it, but . . ."

"Children, it's time I was on my way!" Madame Babin made haste to announce.

"No, no, Mama! Lulu will see you home. . . ."

"I don't need anyone to see me home. I hardly think I run any risks in the street at my age."

Stubbornly, she looked around for her things. As long as Charles didn't seize the opportunity to . . .

"All right, then . . . Good night, Mama. See you on Sunday."

"Good night, children. Don't get up. I'll shut the door properly."

They didn't want to leave him in peace! For twenty years, for more than twenty years, nothing had happened, apart from Marie. Never had there been an unexpected visitor, never a surprise in the mailbox, never anything that had changed their everyday life one iota.

Now, it was one thing on top of another. . . . There was Henri. There was the five hundred thousand francs. He was being rushed. . . . He wasn't being given time to get his thoughts in order. . . . And what were they going to bother him with now?

"Listen, Charles . . . Don't make that face. The poor girl can't help it."

It was clear from the way Camille was acting that Laurence was talking about her. Her, too? He could not help studying her figure. Laurence understood.

"It's not what you think! She's engaged. . . . She was planning to tell us one of these days. . . . Today, *he* told her *he* had accepted a job in Egypt. . . . Tell him yourself, Camille."

Camille was all at sea.

"He's my teacher . . ." she stammered. "He didn't know. They offered him this job all of a sudden. A teaching job in a big French school in Cairo . . . He'll earn three times what he gets here, even with the shorthand classes he gives in the evenings."

Suddenly she began quietly crying and turned her face to the stove. At the same moment, Lulu stood up and went out, so quickly that her exit was almost unnoticed.

"Where's she going?"

To her room, the door of which soon slammed.

Sugaring her coffee, Laurence came to Camille's rescue.

"You see . . . there's no way he can come all that way back to get married. . . . He has to sail in a month. . . . Of course, it's all somewhat of a rush. . . . But it seems he's a sincere, honest young man. Camille says she's sure of him, and of herself. What do you think?"

He was at a loss to know what to answer, or even what attitude to adopt. He looked at them vaguely. Was that all? Camille wanting to get married?

His answer made Laurence burst out laughing:

"What do we have to do?" was all he asked.

"First, we have to get him here, so he can ask for her hand. Then, we have to publish the banns, right away, if they're going to get married within a month. Everyone will get to work on the trousseau. . . . Perhaps it would be a good idea if you found out something about him. That's easy, because he

119

has only his mother, who lives on a small pension. . . . She may join them later."

"All right . . ."

"I thought he could come on Sunday. . . . That way he'd get to meet the whole family."

"Yes . . ."

Laurence made a sign to her daughter.

"Kiss your father!"

Camille obeyed, kissing Charles and stammering:

"Thanks, Papa."

Then she, too, ran up to her room. Lulu was already in bed, which almost never happened. Camille thought she was crying. She crept toward her and touched her face to see if it was wet.

"What's the matter?" asked Lulu calmly. "Why don't you turn the light on?"

"I thought . . ."

She switched on the light and saw that her sister's eyes were open and staring at her.

"Is it because of me?" asked Camille anxiously.

"What?"

"I don't know. . . . Does it upset you?"

"That you're getting married? . . . That's a good one."

"What, then? . . . Is it because of what Mauricette said before?"

It had certainly been tactless of Mauricette. Why tell Lulu that she had seen Georges with another girl?

Especially since Lulu had also seen him. He had deliberately walked past the shoeshop and stopped in front of the window.

"You must know by now he's not the boy for you. . . . Stop thinking about him."

"I've already stopped. . . . I couldn't care less."

Not to mention that all he had found to replace her was

the doctor's daughter! Everyone knew about her! She was only sixteen, and crazy. She would slip declarations of love in boys' mailboxes. Michel's mother had caught her at it and told her a few home truths.

As for older men, married or single, she would stare at them in such a way that they would be embarrassed.

With the doctor's daughter, at least, they could turn the light off at Georges's friend's or not turn it off! She wasn't the sort of girl to be upset by something like that.

"You know Papa didn't say a thing."

"What was he supposed to say?" sighed Lulu, turning to the wall.

"It's strange to think that I won't be sleeping with you in this room any more. . . ."

"Turn the light off, will you?"

Downstairs, Charles and Laurence were still dawdling. They did not speak. Laurence studied her husband. She wanted to ask him about the five thousand francs, but decided that now was not the time.

"Are you coming up?"

They went to bed. The house was completely dark.

As for Mauricette, who was out dancing with her count, she was off on a new tack. She could not understand why she had never thought of it before. Her friend simply had to ask for a divorce! Hadn't she been a virgin when he met her? Wasn't she as good as his wife?

She had no idea yet how to go about it, but she began to look at him in a new way, and her laughter tonight was more nervous than usual.

"Are you asleep, Charles?"

He did not answer her. They had been in bed a long time, but he was not asleep. Mauricette was already back. The noise

of the trains had stopped. Laurence, who usually fell asleep
quickly, sighed from time to time.

Even though he had not replied, she could sense that he
was not asleep either. She waited a little while longer. She did
not touch him. He always lay on the very edge of the bed,
nearly always with one arm dangling.

"Have you thought that now there'll be two gone?"

A tremor ran through the bed. He realized that Laurence
was crying.

"After that . . ."

She left the thought unfinished. The other two . . .

". . . when we're all by ourselves . . ."

She no longer tried to hide her sobs. And something happened, the most extraordinary thing that had ever happened
in their life together. Laurence's hand groped among the moist
sheets until it felt her husband's flesh; and she touched him,
timidly, as if to reassure herself, as if to . . .

It had suddenly got much colder, and the streets, which had
been dark, turned a harsh white from the frost; everything
seemed wider and emptier, sounds carried a longer distance,
and footsteps echoed as people walked, their hands in their
pockets, their noses red, little clouds in front of their faces
when they breathed out.

Mademoiselle Thérèse had a cold. She was constantly
blowing her nose, and she came up to the office to put her
handkerchiefs near the gas stove to dry.

What was there so odd about Charles that bothered her?
She threw curious little troubled glances at him and asked him
stupid questions:

"Haven't you been upstairs this morning?"

Why should he have gone upstairs? Henri had not asked
for him. One of the maids had come down, but only to see if

he was there. She had reappeared in the afternoon, then again the next morning. Henri must be worried, asking from time to time:

"Is Charles downstairs?"

Albert dropped in on his way to a lecture, but did not come into the glass cage. Nor did Martine, who always took the private staircase.

The previous evening, Arthur had come to the house. He had shaken both his brother-in-law's hands and had kept them in his own.

"You know, Charles, what you did . . ."

Charles had not done it for him, or for anybody, but to amuse himself, almost as a challenge.

"I'd like everything to be in order. I think we should sign papers. . . ."

As if he would ever pay it back, with or without papers!

The women had already started on the trousseau. The sewing machine hummed until midnight. There were pieces of material everywhere, and the table was littered with gray paper patterns, which were simply brushed to one side at mealtimes.

When, on the fourth day, Henri came down to the office, Charles had not yet made up his mind. He could tell immediately, from the way his brother-in-law looked at him, that he was waiting for an answer, even as he pretended to ask questions about the business.

It was amazing how much Henri had changed in so short a time. Could a man lose so much weight in a few days? His jacket and, especially, his waistcoat seemed to have become too loose, as if his stomach had collapsed. His cheeks were hollow, and his eyes still had rings under them.

But what was most striking was the cautious way he walked or made the slightest gesture, as though afraid that if he made a sudden movement, he might break something inside.

"Have the bills been paid?"

"Yes, all of them. I've been to the bank. . . . The Barmat business is settled. . . ."

Henri had not sat down. He had surely already looked in the safe, so he knew that Charles, although he had been given permission, had taken nothing for himself.

It was all beyond him. Perhaps Charles was putting off an explanation until later, when he was feeling better? Or perhaps he expected the initiative to come from his brother-in-law?

Seeing Charles attending to the accounts, in his old jacket, it was possible to believe that nothing had changed. He had always been like that, had always seemed like someone separated from the outside world by an invisible membrane. Weren't deaf people rather the same?

Henri had a short walk around the warehouses, without daring to light his cigar; the doctor had forbidden him to smoke. Then he opened the door and walked around the office, without looking his brother-in-law in the face. He shuffled papers, searching for something that was not there, still hoping that the other would speak. But Charles did not even look up.

Did he still hate Henri as much as ever? Sometimes he almost felt sorry for him. During the days of waiting, especially in the mornings, when there were frost flowers on the windowpanes and he slowly opened the mail, he had occasionally decided, or almost decided, to get it over with.

It would be easy, and he would still have the advantage. He would declare:

"That's how I got the five hundred thousand francs. I'm keeping them. . . ."

He could simply go away. With all that money, couldn't he do whatever he liked?

At the last moment, he could not go through with it. All day long, he busied himself with invoices and bills, some of them due after three or six months, some of them needing legal action for collection. In the afternoon, sitting on a chair higher than the others, he wrote diligently in the ledger, never making a mistake, even though he did not stop thinking his own thoughts for a single second.

He had understood the whole story ever since Sylvie's second letter. It had not been difficult to figure out; he had the firm's accounts at his disposal and he had long suspected his brother-in-law of having played a dirty trick on his partner.

One evening when his daughters had all gone out and Laurence was sewing, he had sat down at the roll-top desk and used the colored inks.

Ever since he was little, he had been fond of working elaborately with colored inks and watercolors, and it was for his own pleasure that he had drawn Marie's school maps.

On this occasion, he used a ruler to draw letters, like printed letters but sloping to the right.

You think you're clever.

He had no idea why he signed it *Popaul.*

He did not smile. He worked as conscientiously at these notes as he had at the maps.

When you've finally made your riches, your bubble will burst.

Popaul

He never spoke as crudely as that, and it was hard to know where it had come from.

All day long, in the office with Henri, he treated him as his boss and never dared to be familiar with him. Then, in the evening, he enjoyed himself with his inks, writing certain words in red to make them more threatening.

125

You sacked a warehouseman for stealing two cans of sardines, and yet you stole the whole business.

Popaul

When the first note arrived in the mail, Henri read it in front of him, but after that he stuffed the envelopes in his pocket whenever he saw the address written in square letters.

You can always run after Sylvie. She isn't at her old address any more.

Popaul

Charles decided to continue doing this for a long time. It was pure joy, without any ulterior motive. It never crossed his mind to do what Sylvie had tried to do: profit by what he knew and extort money from Henri.

What did he need money for? He had never had any great desire for it. Besides, he had enough. He had long been stealing money from Henri, on principle, as a sort of revenge.

At first, a long time ago, when Marie was still little, he had taken small amounts from the till, five or ten francs to buy candy or a toy or a birthday or name-day present.

It was easy. Money flowed like water in the business, and you had only to dip your hand in and take it.

One evening, after he switched the light off, he took a thousand-franc note by mistake. He hid it, because it would have been impossible to spend it all at once. And what could he have spent it on?

It became a habit, an addiction. Since he used the attic as his darkroom, he hid the money there. He kept a constant store of it, like a puppy hiding bones and hard bread.

He had always been a hoarder, but for no particular purpose. Little by little, he built up a fund of about thirty thousand francs. He thought of sending it to Marie, and would have if he knew her address.

Once, when Henri bought some shares and bonds at the stock exchange and asked him to deposit the certificates in the bank, Charles kept one of them for himself.

Suddenly this certificate became redeemable at five hundred thousand francs. Charles learned about it by consulting the financial journals Henri subscribed to.

Had his brother-in-law kept a list of his holdings? Or was the list Charles drew up for him the only one he had?

This was what had put him in such a state, one winter evening. All at once, he stopped thinking about his notes written with a ruler and colored ink.

He had five hundred thousand francs! He drew it from the bank. He brought it home. After twenty years, he could transform the life of the household from top to bottom, as if with a magic wand. Laurence always talked to him about the gas bill. Lulu fitted shoes on peasant women. Mauricette slept with her boss so that she could go to fashionable restaurants and get a fur coat, which she could wear only in secret.

And he had five hundred thousand francs! The streets were dark and full of rain and reflections on the sidewalks and people running from one shop to another, and he could buy whatever he wanted!

He bought provisions. In order to lock himself in the attic. To have time to think.

And there he had heard Laurence and the girls; he had guessed what they were thinking from the confused conversation that reached him through the chimney flues. On Sunday, he had heard the family gathering and the voice of Paul, the Babin oracle.

He had taken his time. There was no need to hurry. He had become powerful, more powerful even than Dionnet!

What difference did it make if everyone downstairs thought

he was mad? Occasionally he heard Laurence's nervous laughter, and knew what she was thinking.

Unfortunately, just as with this business of Camille and her fiancé, things had happened too quickly. He had not been given time to savor the situation.

Henri received an impatient telegram from Sylvie:

IF NO IMMEDIATE RESPONSE TO MY LETTERS I WILL DO WHAT I HAVE TO.

SYLVIE

All at once, Henri understood. Had he never suspected Charles? Charles, who behaved like a mouse nibbling cheese? Now everything became clear! He went running, interrupted Paul and Laurence, needing to have his mind set at rest, come what may.

It had made him ill. He was still ill. He seemed uncomfortable. He wandered around restlessly. And, for the first time in his life, he walked through the warehouses ten times over without making a single unpleasant remark.

Now Charles could say to him:

"You're offering me money to keep quiet. Well, I've already helped myself. I stole a bond from you, and now it's worth five hundred thousand francs. . . ."

It would make Henri ill again, but less so. To think that one of his bonds . . . five hundred thousand francs . . . And to think that he, the clever thief, could have been robbed without being aware of it . . .

It would make him ill, though in a different way. But also relieved. He would be back on firm ground, solid and sure of himself as head of the business.

He would certainly demand that Charles leave. It was uncomfortable to live every day with someone who knew too much, especially about such unpleasant secrets.

And then?

That was the crux of it. What would become of Charles then, even with five hundred thousand francs? Would they no longer jump when they heard his key in the lock? Would the girls no longer stop singing or squabbling? Would Laurence suddenly feel as much at ease with him as she did with Paul and Céline? Would Lulu . . . ?

Everything would be exactly the same! That was the conclusion he had reached. Perhaps in a slightly more comfortable house, but the family would soon make that as untidy as always. Mauricette would not need her count any more, but she would find something else. And Marie would still not return.

At most, they would no longer see Paul sitting by the fire, with his pipe and his dark clothes, because, as he was fond of saying, he did not like the smell of rich people.

Laurence did not like it either, not Céline, nor anyone in the family. Nor did Charles. He had never felt at ease in the Dionnets' house, on the rare occasions he was invited there.

So?

He said nothing. He remained the same. He did his job as meticulously as ever, because that was his nature and he enjoyed it. He was robbing Henri, but he would work three nights running to track down a discrepancy of two francs in the accounts. He hated Henri, but the thought of leaving his glass cage made him feel sick. In the mornings, he watched Henri lingering in the warehouses, hesitating to enter the office, doing so only under some pretext, and waiting for the opportunity to throw Charles an anxious glance.

Charles could have looked him in the eye, sneered, lighted a cigarette—though he was a nonsmoker—and blown the smoke in his face, or else put his feet up on the desk. He had thought about it. He had considered all the alternatives open to him. The very reason he had locked himself in the attic for several days was to savor these prospects.

But in the end he merely murmured respectfully:

"Good morning, Dionnet."

Then he talked about some coffee purchase or an insolvent customer. Humbly! Humbly in precisely the way that infuriated Henri.

What could Henri offer him to keep him quiet and make him go away for good? A hundred thousand? Two hundred thousand? He was a man who would bargain despite everything.

And then?

Then it would be over. The old life would resume, with a little extra money. As Laurence had said, there would soon be two gone. The fiancé was coming tomorrow. Mauricette and Lulu would be left. . . .

And then?

He wished it were colder. He loved winters when ice drifted on the Seine, and summers when crops were scorched by the sun, and storms that caused lots of damage, because then he would feel totally safe and sound in his glass cage.

Henri was melting! He was becoming almost human! He even spoke sometimes in a voice that could have been called soft, but it was only because he was lowering his voice for fear of reawakening his heart trouble.

"What's that?" he had asked, pointing at two of Mademoiselle Thérèse's handkerchiefs drying in front of the gas stove.

"Handkerchiefs," Charles had replied.

It was obvious they were a woman's handkerchiefs. Previously, Henri would have flown into a rage and cursed and threatened to fire the guilty party.

Instead, he had gone away, his fingers in his waistcoat pockets, a gap between his waistcoat and his stomach.

Charles would say nothing. That was the best thing. He was not overfond of Camille, who was too much of a Babin, already fat and flabby like her mother and her aunts, but, without telling anyone, he would send her a little money in Cairo, twenty or thirty thousand francs, and nobody would know where it came from. That would make it all the funnier!

As for the rest of it, he had time. He amused himself by arriving at the office ten minutes late and leaving five minutes early. Mademoiselle Thérèse looked anxiously at her watch, sure that there was something wrong with it.

Who would be coming tomorrow for the engagement party? Wasn't it ironic that it should be Camille who was leaving, the only one of the girls who would have liked to stay, lounging around in slippers while her grandmother came to see her one day a week, giving birth surrounded by her aunts, pushing the child in its carriage as she paid them each a visit . . . ?

She was going to live in Egypt!

It made her cry, with joy and despair. She sewed from morning to night. She had left her job at the corset-maker's and seemed to be apologizing to her parents and sisters for no longer bringing in any money to the family. And yet there was still four hundred and ninety-five thousand francs on top of the cabinet in the attic.

As for Lulu, she too spent her evenings sewing.

"Aren't you going to the movies?" her mother would ask in surprise.

"Why should I go to the movies?"

And all evening she would keep her teeth clenched, except to ask for the tape measure or the scissors or thread of one color or another.

Chapter 9

THEY ALL, ESPECIALLY LAURENCE, BLAMED THEMSELVES LATER for having lived through those weeks badly, without paying attention, worrying, agitated, and in a foul mood. But what could they have done, with everything conspiring against them?

First, the weather. Charles, who loved memorable events, must have been happy. The newspapers had to go back to the middle of the last century to find a year like this. For three or four days on end, rain fell in torrents, without a stop, and it was impossible to run even as far as Madame Josse's. Then, one morning, they woke to see a livid sky and people in the street who seemed to be performing some grotesque dance, but were merely trying to walk on the ice that covered everything.

Sunday was a day of rain, and at times it drummed so loudly on the glass roof of the kitchen that it was impossible to hear what anyone was saying. They had set up the table for afternoon tea in the front room, and there was another table, in the kitchen, for the children. Céline had brought hers, and they could be heard running up and down the stairs. Poor Céline felt embarrassed, and tried in vain to keep them quiet.

The fiancé's name was Hugon, Pierre Hugon, and he remained in his seat near Camille, a little behind her. Perhaps he was dazed to find himself among so many people. Camille had, of course, explained to him all the ins and outs of the family, but every time the bell rang he probably wondered how many more would be arriving.

Arthur, who had come in his truck, was determined to make everyone try it out, despite the rain and the wind, which lifted the tarpaulin like the wings of a crow.

As for Paul, he seemed to be putting the newcomer through a sort of examination, on behalf of the family. Hugon remained patient and answered calmly and meticulously, although he was a little embarrassed that it was Paul who was center stage and that nobody seemed to care about Charles Dupeux.

Things almost went wrong, however. Hugon remarked, as they were talking about the ceremony:

"I must go and see the parish priest tomorrow."

Everyone felt a storm coming. They did not dare look at Paul, who was fanatically anticlerical, like his father, who had boasted of not having had any of his children baptized.

"Excuse me . . . are you planning to get married in church? . . . Do you mean to say you're a Catholic?"

"Personally, I have no religious convictions. But my mother would be very unhappy if her only son didn't get married in church."

"Leave him alone, Paul," Laurence tried to cut in.

Paul fell silent, only to return to it a quarter of an hour later. It was not as though the afternoon was spoiled, but there was nevertheless a certain unease.

And it was the very next day that . . . yes, the night of Monday to Tuesday . . . The weather had changed, going from rainy black to icy white, and it was almost impossible to heat the kitchen because of that damned glass roof, which was the despair of Laurence.

Suddenly, in the middle of the night, they heard a scream. Then the door of Charles and Laurence's bedroom opened, and Lulu came in, in her pajamas, barefoot, and with her hair disheveled. She seemed like a madwoman or a sleepwalker.

"Fire! Fire!" she kept repeating.

"Charles!" cried Laurence, shaking her husband.

Camille ran in, more calmly.

"It's just opposite," she said.

Everyone got up, but only Lulu did not seem to be fully awake. From her room, they could see red in the sky, quite close by, and hear people running in the street, then the breathless bell of the fire engine.

"Put something on, children, or you'll all catch cold," warned Laurence. "Camille, make your sister something to drink. She's as white as a sheet. . . ."

It was the first time they realized how high-strung Lulu was, and how much she was still a child. She must have waked up and seen the reflection of the flames on the ceiling of her room. She was still shaken by it. The floor was ice-cold under her bare feet. Mauricette wrapped herself in a bedspread.

The fire had broken out at Martin's. He was the cabinetmaker who had his workshop behind the houses opposite. The people in those houses could be seen rushing around their rooms, gathering up their most precious possessions and carrying them out into the street.

It was impossible to go back to bed. More firemen were arriving. The sensible thing was to get dressed. The first to do so was Mauricette, who then left the house. Nobody had thought of checking the time, and they were quite surprised when, before long, the pale light of dawn appeared in the sky.

Sparks were fluttering against the front of the house. Neighbors were helping poor Martin to move out whatever could still be salvaged. They could see him, a huge man with gray hair and a long nose. Already it was being said that he was not insured. Barely two years had passed since he had set up on his own, after having worked for other people all his life.

They made coffee. Lulu did not go to work that morning. Everybody was tired, their faces drawn. About ten o'clock, the firemen coiled their hoses, and the street returned to normal, but something unexpected happened: the whole street was without water. Perhaps because of the cold, a big main had burst, and a trench would have to be dug in the road to repair it. It fell to a policeman to go from door to door and inform the residents that, while waiting, they could get water from the railroad company, just fifty yards from the grade crossing.

That was how the misfortune occurred, stupidly. Laurence went there with two pails. It was her washday. She had put on her clogs. Right at the corner was a large patch of ice. Laurence slipped on it and, to her great surprise, was unable to get up again.

Camille, who was sewing, gave a start when the bell rang. She went to open the door, and there was her mother, being carried by two strangers and one of the neighbors.

It was only a sprain, but the shock of the fall, coupled, no doubt, with the cold, had affected her so much that it was quite a while before she regained consciousness.

Laurence out of action at a time like this, with barely three weeks left to make Camille's trousseau and get everything ready for the wedding! All the girls needed dresses. They had to call in Mademoiselle Chantraine, the dressmaker, who smelled bad and never dreamed of getting anything for herself. Everything had to be handed to her, and she had to be waited on from morning to night.

Laurence was installed in the wicker armchair, her bad leg propped up on another chair.

To make matters worse, it was the end of the year, and the whole town was in a state of excitement. The shops had window displays anticipating the holidays. In the afternoons, especially around five, it was almost impossible to move on the narrow sidewalks, and there were as many people out on the days of frost as on the days of heavy rain.

At Dionnet's, there had been a terrible scene. Martine wanted to go on a winter-sport holiday with two other girls and three young men, two of them English. They intended to stay in a chalet high in the mountains, and she had already bought her clothes and all the equipment.

"Either your brother goes with you, or you don't go!" decided Henri, who at times let his daughter do whatever she liked and at other times was strict.

But Albert could not go with her.

"Too bad! You can go another time."

"And I say I'm going!" said Martine calmly. "I'm old enough to take care of myself. . . . You can try to lock me in, like mother, but I'll climb out the window. . . ."

He had not thought she would, but she had, in fact, gone—with what money, nobody knew.

Elise had seized the opportunity to go on a binge, and trade was at its busiest at this time of year.

Where was there time for any of them to bother about the others? Every evening, on the stroke of eight, Hugon, who had already given up his shorthand classes, rang the bell. He always seemed to be apologizing. Every evening he brought candy, which he placed discreetly on a corner of the table. After greeting everyone, he went and sat down next to, and a little behind, Camille, who would be sewing.

He tended to be too gentle, too well brought up. He never contradicted anyone. Whenever Camille needed something, he was the one who rushed to get it, and during the four days that the water shortage lasted, he was the one who went to the railroad company to fill the pails.

Nobody paid any attention to whether Mauricette went out or not. A week went by without anyone noticing. They had to hire a charwoman for the Saturday cleaning, and every now and again, in the morning, Paul came and sat in the kitchen, but hardly spoke.

Charles, who had never bothered much about the house, did not have a part in any of it. He was still playing his fascinating game, keeping his eye on Henri. They still had not had it out.

Would the two of them ever have it out? Henri was looking more like his old self. Although he had probably not put on any weight, he had regained the solidity and the self-confidence he had always had as an important employer. He finally made a scene about Mademoiselle Thérèse's handkerchiefs, which she was still drying by the gas stove, and even threatened to fire her despite her twenty years with the company.

After that, it was impossible to tell if she was blowing her nose because she had a cold or because she was crying.

Ten or twenty times a day, Henri went into the office, and each time the same game was played. Charles would not look up. Henri would cough and relight his cigar—he had stopped following the doctor's advice so strictly. When he opened his mouth, it was to inquire about some unimportant matter.

He didn't dare! And yet Charles was quite insignificant— a short, dull, badly dressed, even puny fellow.

Occasionally a shiver ran down Charles's spine, and he thought:

What's to stop him from trying to kill me?

After all, he was the only person preventing his brother-in-law from calmly enjoying the fortune and the position he had acquired. As long as he was around . . .

And didn't the fact that he was so humble, so self-effacing, so much the lowly employee, the poor relation, make it all the more unbearable?

He would deliberately lower his eyes, hunch his shoulders, and speak in a respectful tone.

No doubt later, after Camille's wedding, he would decide what to do. They had all started to say "after Camille's wedding," as if it were an event that would mark a decisive break in their lives.

The letter arrived when Laurence was already walking a little, but only indoors; she was not yet able to put her shoes on. It was Lulu who gave it to her sister, to whom it was addressed. Camille, after first hesitating to open it, cried:

"It's from Marie!"

It was morning. Charles had not left for work yet. Camille had to read the letter aloud:

My dear sister,

I've read in the Gazette de Rouen *that you're getting married, and I'd like to be one of the first to congratulate you and wish you luck. It's almost as if I'd had a premonition. Every time I happen to see the* Gazette de Rouen, *which is quite seldom, I carefully read the births, deaths, and marriages, and yesterday I came across your name.*

I assume you're happy and all the family are happy for you.

As for me, I'm quite content. For the past six months I've been living with my friend, running a small hotel in the forest of Orléans. My friend used to work at the Ritz as a cook. He's a really decent sort. He loves me very much and the only reason he hasn't married me yet is because his wife is doing all she can to oppose the divorce. Too bad if our parents read this letter. They'll jump to all sorts of conclusions!

Charles (his name's Charles, like our father) had some savings. We borrowed fifty thousand francs to buy the hotel and we've already got a very nice clientele, especially in the hunting season, all bankers and businessmen.

The work is hard but pleasant, and I really like it, es-

138

pecially since we're meeting such interesting people all day long.

If you've got a moment to spare, what with your wedding and all the commotion there must be at home, do drop me a line with all the news. What's Lulu up to? Is she still just as thin and is Mauricette just as proud? If I know Mama, she can't have changed much. Is our father still working for Uncle Henri?

I often think of you all and look forward to hearing from you. With all my love,

Marie

Laurence burst out laughing.

"So now she's got a restaurant!" she cried.

And all morning, she seemed to be talking to herself. When Paul came and took his usual seat in the kitchen, she could not help saying:

"Do you remember what you told me about Mama?"

"What do you mean?"

"I mean, what she was doing before she got married. . . ."

She glanced at her daughter, who was sewing at the machine, and took advantage of the noise drowning her voice to tell her brother:

"Marie's doing the exact same thing. . . . But for herself . . . Read her letter . . . Camille, what have you done with Marie's letter?"

Then, in the last week, came another worry. Laurence was determined to have Henri at the wedding, but for that she had to get Paul to agree to sit at the same table as his brother-in-law.

"But I tell you, you won't have to speak to him! There'll be so many people there, you'll never come face to face with

139

him. . . . What does it matter if he's there? . . . Just ignore him."

Paul listened to the arguments and nodded, but said nothing. Laurence asked Camille to back her up.

Then there was a real bombshell in the last week, when nothing was ready, all the arrangements still had to be made, and that old cow of a dressmaker was in the house from morning till night, making it impossible for them to talk freely, because she was a gossip and a mischief-maker.

Only Bobinec would burst dramatically into someone's house the way he did and announce at the top of his voice, without caring who heard him:

"Guess where Arthur is!"

There was no way of knowing if he was bringing good or bad news. His tragic voice was comical, and his comic voice was sad.

"How should I know?"

He replied, with a sweeping gesture:

"He's in jail!"

It was true. Arthur had been in jail since the previous evening. The police had come for him when he was in the middle of dinner. He had understood immediately, whereas his poor wife, who had no idea what was going on, had got into a terrible state.

"Paul's with the examining magistrate," explained Bobinec. "We really must get Arthur out of there. . . ."

That morning, in a village, he had knocked down a child with his truck, the truck Charles had paid for. Arthur had panicked and, instead of stopping and picking the victim up off the ground, had accelerated like a madman, unaware that a woman, standing on her doorstep, had taken down his number.

He learned of the child's death only when he was at the magistrate's after his arrest. Earlier, he said nothing about it to anyone, and spent the day wandering from bar to bar.

140

"Do you think Henri can do anything? He knows a lot of people."

Laurence, who had recovered from her sprain, rushed to Dionnet's. She went up to see her sister first, but Elise insulted her irrationally through the door, shouting that they were a family of beggars and she had had enough of them.

She went down to the office, where she saw Charles bent over his ledger.

"Arthur's in prison!" she told him.

And he replied, as if it were quite natural:

"Well, well."

"He ran over a child with his truck. . . . Isn't Henri here?"

She caught sight of him, near some wagons that were being loaded. As she walked toward him, she began to cry.

"Listen, Henri, we really must do something. . . . Four days before Camille's wedding! . . . Arthur's in jail. . . . He . . ."

Henri telephoned a judge he knew, whose daughter was a friend of Martine's. The judge replied that there was nothing that could be done.

When Laurence told him about it, Paul sneered bitterly:

"If he were rich like your brother-in-law, they'd let him out on bail. . . . But he's only a poor fellow who has to earn his living and feed his family. . . ."

"Promise me you'll come on Saturday, Paul."

He refused to promise. He did not say yes or no.

"Those people disgust me!"

And there was Hugon in the middle of all this, still calm and gentle, still coming every evening and sitting in the same place, sometimes going a whole hour without speaking, if nobody asked him anything.

"After the wedding, we'll have to see about Lulu," said Laurence, perhaps two days before the ceremony. "She hasn't been the same since the fire. She doesn't seem to have recovered from the shock. . . ."

And that was the only mention of the subject. There were too many things to think about.

Then all at once the day and the hour arrived, even though they thought they still had plenty of time. They all got dressed up, with the doors open, so that they could call each other, because everyone needed help, with a missing stitch here, a hook there.

When the car pulled up in front of the door, Laurence began to cry, for no reason. Immediately, Camille began to cry too, even harder, and they climbed into the car with red eyes.

It was a day of frost. The silk and satin dresses were light, and they should have been wearing fur coats. Only Mauricette had one. She told them a girl friend had lent it to her.

Madame Hugon, Pierre's mother, was a cripple and could not come. She lived in the suburbs of Paris. Hugon had chosen as his witness a bookkeeping teacher, who was dressed in a dinner jacket and had cut himself shaving. Camille's witness was Paul, who refused to dress any differently from usual.

It was a Saturday. In the streets, they saw people in winter sports clothes walking to the station, with skis on their shoulders. At the last moment, pale and bleary-eyed, Elise had got up, and her two maids had helped her to dress.

Paul's daughter, Berthe, and Lulu were bridesmaids, both in blue. As luck would have it, Berthe had a large pimple on her nose.

The one who most escaped notice was Charles. Although he was there, he was invisible. Curiously, nobody bothered about him. At the town hall, he got mixed up in another wedding and had difficulty extricating himself.

The hall was ice-cold. They had a long wait. There was a society wedding taking place, with a whole line of cars outside. Henri and Paul pretended not to know each other, and the fates seemed to be wickedly conspiring to throw them together time after time.

Clémence could not think of anything but her husband, in jail, and she talked about him to everyone.

In church, Paul made sure they were all aware that he wanted to stay aloof from this make-believe, and he followed his signature on the register with three Masonic dots.

The reception was at the Cardinal Restaurant. There were three wedding parties, in three different rooms. The red of the lobsters stood out against the white of the tablecloths.

As early as four, the bridal pair was due to catch the train for Paris, where they would visit Hugon's mother, and then leave the next morning for Marseilles, to set sail.

Camille looked at her mother, her sisters, and her aunts as if she wanted to hang on to them. Bobinec secretly read through the topical song he had written, which he planned to sing at the end of the meal.

Charles, too, had prepared something. The idea had come to him in bed the previous night. He had slipped a hundred thousand-franc notes into an envelope and sealed it. Soon, when the couple were leaving, he would hand the envelope to Hugon and say:

"Don't open it till you get to Cairo."

It amused him to think about it as he watched Henri. He was glad that the day after next, Monday, he would be back in his place in the glass cage, seeing his brother-in-law hanging around him. . . .

Another wedding party must have begun their meal earlier, because they could hear singing and monologues while they were still on the cheese course. Bobinec was impatient. Céline's children, dressed in new clothes, were eating at a little table, with the baby's cradle placed across two chairs. Céline had to go and breast-feed him.

They were all a little afraid of Paul. They knew that at any moment he might launch an onslaught against Henri, or the rich in general, or priests. From time to time, Laurence threw him an imploring look.

The photographer created a diversion. He had come for all three wedding parties. He posed everyone, the children sitting on the floor, then Hugon and the bride on chairs, and the others standing in a semicircle.

"Where's Lulu?" asked Berthe in surprise. She needed the second bridesmaid to balance her in the picture.

They thought she might be in the ladies' room. Berthe went to have a look. The photographer was getting impatient.

No Lulu!

"She must have been feeling tired," said her mother. "She hasn't been the same since the fire. . . ."

"Surely she hasn't gone home alone?"

The photographer went ahead without Lulu. Amid all the commotion, Bobinec sang his song. Elise, who had been drinking despite Henri's stern looks, sobbed and told everyone that she was the best of women. And then it was almost over. The young couple was about to leave. They kissed everyone. They kissed one aunt twice and overlooked another one altogether. The room, which had been too hot earlier, was now freezing cold, because a door had been left open.

Cigars were passed. Céline's children ran all over the place and amused themselves by sliding on the parquet floor as if it were ice, even in the rooms where the other wedding parties were eating.

The confusion had lasted, not just for a few hours, but for weeks. Nobody really knew what was going on. They were feeling their way.

"As long as Paul and Henri . . ."

But there they were, by a window, smoking cigars and calmly discussing something.

Had Camille already left? They looked for her and Hugon. Laurence was downstairs, by the car covered with white flowers that was taking them away.

There was still some liquor left, and Bobinec seized his opportunity. His wife had her hands full with the children and could not keep her eye on him. If he got drunk, nothing would stop him from singing bawdy songs.

There was a detail that Charles noticed: the scornful smile of his daughter Mauricette as she gazed disdainfully at this family gathering.

It was impossible to see everyone at once. Arthur's wife, Clémence, was one of the first to leave, because she had an appointment with a lawyer. Then Henri, carrying Elise off before it was too late.

The chandeliers were lighted. It was time to go, but they lazily dawdled, to the great despair of the waiters. All that was left were some petits fours and a little champagne at the bottom of the bottles. Nobody cared what glass they drank out of. The atmosphere had become as casual as on Sundays in Laurence's kitchen, and they had all forgotten they were dressed up for a wedding.

"What did he say to you?" Paul was asked.

"He spoke to me first. . . . He told me that if we had to put up bail for Arthur, he was willing to do it. . . . Because it's bad for him and his business to have a brother-in-law in jail. . . . I answered . . ."

Madame Babin sat all alone, waiting for it to be over and watching her family's excitement.

"Aren't you cold, Mama?" Céline asked her. "You should have brought a shawl."

"Don't worry about me, child . . . You've all got enough to worry about already. . . ."

Céline paid no attention to this. Her baby was crying. She tried to gather her family together, but she could not get

Bobinec to leave; he was singing his songs in the next room, to much applause and loud laughter.

"Mama . . ." begged Mauricette, pulling her mother's sleeve.

The time had come. They had to go.

"Is your father ready?"

"He's waiting. . . ."

"So am I. . . ."

Once they were in the car, which they had rented, they were quite surprised to find themselves alone together, just the three of them. They said nothing, feeling ill-at-ease. Laurence still felt like crying, doubtless because it was customary at weddings.

It was odd to arrive at the grade crossing by car and wait, although there was only a little way to walk. Madame Josse was watching them through her shop window. Mauricette got out first and searched in her bag for her key. The house was ice-cold. Their voices echoed through it strangely.

Before taking her things off, Laurence went to light the fire in the kitchen, which she did clumsily, because of her good clothes. When the fire did not catch, she grabbed the oilcan and poured out quite a lot.

The smell filled the house.

"Lulu!" Mauricette shouted up the stairs.

There was the sound of doors opening. Mauricette called again:

"Lulu!"

Charles left his overcoat on the coatrack and slowly climbed the stairs. Why was he going up to the third floor?

He opened the attic door. There was a long silence.

"Mauricette!" he finally called softly, leaning over the banister. "Come up here a moment."

She went up, saying:

"What's the matter?"

She fell silent on seeing her father on the landing, his face pale, a finger to his lips.

"Shh!"

And then she saw it. . . . A long, thin, pale-blue figure, without breasts or hips, hanging from the skylight's iron curtain rod . . . A sheath of blue satin and two feet that seemed twisted at right angles to the floor . . .

"Go to your mother and break it to her gently. . . . Don't let her come up here yet. . . ."

Charles was as calm as ever, as blank as ever, and his eyelids appeared transparent.

"Go . . ."

In a garage somewhere, a young man of nineteen named Georges was lying under a car. He, too, was in blue. He looked out from under to check the time. The doctor's daughter was waiting on a street corner, watching the hands of a big electric clock above the traffic policeman.

It was the end of the week, the end of the year. The next day was Sunday, but the shops would be open because of the holidays. People were returning home with packages hidden behind their backs, which they would slip into closets or under beds, in order to spring a surprise.

Train whistles blew. The crossing guard had been provided with a brazier.

Laurence had sprained her leg. Arthur was in jail. Henri and Paul had patched up their quarrel and talked to each other. Camille was gone.

They had certainly noticed—or at least Laurence had— that Lulu had been pale, but they had put off dealing with it until after the wedding.

And now Lulu was dead.

It was too late to call back Camille and her husband. Yes, it was true; she had a husband now!

Marie, in her hotel, had probably not happened to read the *Gazette de Rouen* that day. They forgot to inform her.

Four days after the wedding, the family got together again for the funeral. Then they gathered in Laurence's kitchen, with Paul once more apparently in charge and Charles unnoticed in the background.

This time, it was a day of heavy rain. At the cemetery it was almost impossible to reach the new section, with its sparsely scattered slimy tombstones, where the coffin was buried. This time, there was no priest, because of the suicide, and Paul had nothing to grumble about.

When everyone had left, there was only Mauricette in the house. Mauricette, who . . .

But she had changed her plans. Or else things were not working out as she had hoped with her count. She wrote to Marie. Marie replied:

"If you want to . . ."

Mauricette announced:

"I'm going to work for Marie."

She was quite capable of stealing Marie's friend from her. It was Mauricette's nature. She was interested only in other women's men.

As for Charles, he had faded so much that he suddenly looked his age, forty-eight, and it became obvious that his hair was not blond, but gray. They had always said "ash-blond."

Laurence complained of rheumatism and said it was due to that damned kitchen with the glass roof, which was too hot in summer and freezing cold in winter.

My dear parents . . . wrote Camille. From Cairo!

Arthur was sentenced to six months' imprisonment. The truck was confiscated. Bobinec, thanks to his performance at the neighboring wedding party, had been invited to other weddings and was building up a reputation, so that he spent less and less time on his painting-and-decorating business.

Martine returned with a boy she had chosen as her future husband, and she herself fixed the amount of her dowry.

Charles continued to go every morning to the Place du Vieux-Marché and take his seat in the glass cage, in his old jacket and green eyeshade.

Elise died, and Martine claimed her mother's share. She settled somewhere in the south of England and affected an English accent.

As for Albert, he took advantage of having failed an exam to enlist in a camel regiment, and from Syria he sent poems to avant-garde journals.

The house on the Place du Vieux-Marché, which had swallowed up three old houses, was almost deserted.

The Dupeux house was deserted too, except for Laurence and Charles.

Laurence still lingered in the morning over her coffee and her newspaper. She still went out in her worn old shoes to shop in the local places, and bought food for the evening at Josse's.

"What about your daughter in Egypt?" she was asked from time to time.

"She's expecting. . . . It's a pity it's so far away. . . ."

So far that it was quite impossible to imagine how things were there. They did not know what to make of the photos they were sent, in which Camille and her husband were dressed in white in the middle of winter.

It was Charles, again, who changed the least as he got older. In the evenings, he wrote long letters to Camille and Marie.

"Give my regards to Mauricette . . ."

But his real life was in the office, in his cage, where he sat and waited, saying nothing, stubbornly persisting in saying nothing, watching his brother-in-law die slowly, ever so slowly, of fear.

Nieul, October 1939